UFOs
PROPHECY
AND THE END OF TIME

Sean Casteel

INNER LIGHT PUBLICATIONS

UFOS, PROPHECY
and the
END OF TIME

ISBN: 1892062356

Author, Sean Casteel
Editorial Director, Timothy G. Beckley
Art & Editorial Consultant, Carol Ann Rodriguez
Cover & Graphics, Tim Swartz

Photos from the files of ISRAEL UFO RESEARCH

members.tripod.com/-ufoisrael.html - or do a search on www.google.com

Free weekly newsletter - www.ConspiracyJournal.com

For foreign and reprint rights contact:
Global Communications, Box 753, New Brunswick, NJ 08903

CONTENTS

Chapter 1 – The Wake Up Call   **5**

Chapter 2 – The Aliens In Scripture   **11**

Chapter 3 – Good And Evil Among The Abductees   **22**

Chapter 4 – Dr. R. Leo Sprinkle And Benevolent Aliens   **39**

Chapter 5 – Heaven's Gate: How Some True Believers Got It Wrong   **48**

Chapter 6 – The Meaning Of Prophecy   **61**

Chapter 7 – Gary Stearman And Predictions From The Bible   **67**

Chapter 8 – UFOs and the Military—Doomsday Scenario?   **77**

Chapter 9 – Diane Tessman: An Inspired Voice From The Future   **87**

Chapter 10 – Judith Bluestone Polich: Ancient Prophecies For A New World   **99**

Chapter 11 – Th e Astrological Forecasts Of Dr. Louis Turi   **109**

Chapter 12 – Does Whitley Strieber Have The Key?   **118**

Chapter 13 – Dr. Joe Lewels: Mysteries From On High   **126**

Chapter 14 – The Mid-East Crisis And The Future Of The Holy Land   **131**

Chapter 15 – A Cry To Prophesy   **135**

About the Author and Acknowledgments – **140**

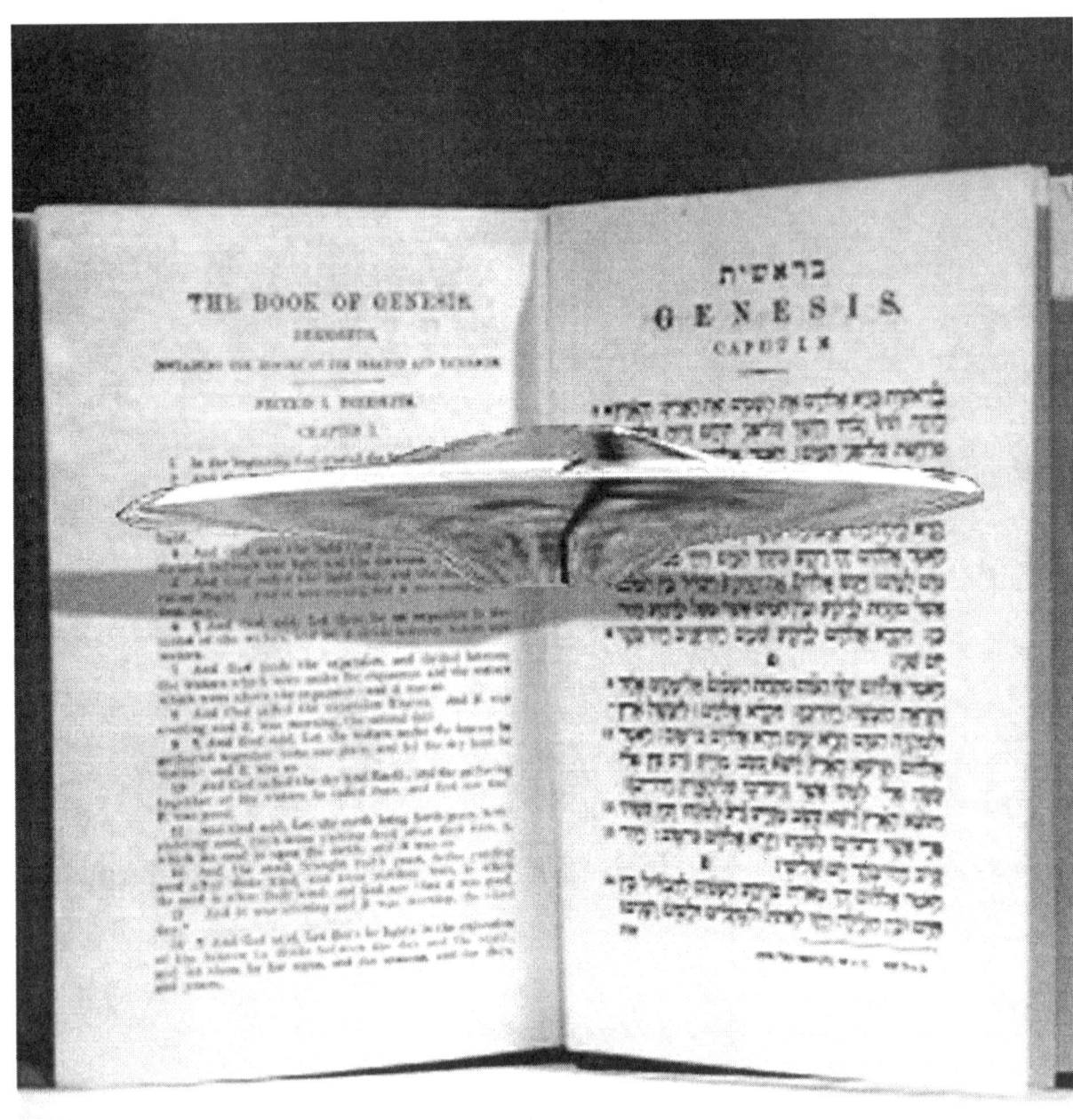

Chapter One
The Wake Up Call

In the first days following the attack, people were already arguing that the events were the fulfillment of prophecy, both in the Bible and in the work of Nostradamus. While the prophecies of course strengthened the idea that something close to the End of the World was happening, they also provided a kind of reassurance that such terrible events are not left to chance, or to the whims of a few madmen with a lust for death.

Isaiah 30:25 was one prophecy quoted at the time. It reads, "And upon every lofty mountain and every high hill there will be brooks running with water, in the day of the great slaughter, when the towers fall."

You wake up slowly, turning and tossing a little, unwilling to get up just yet. You smell the coffee coming from the kitchen, but it isn't enough to motivate you to arise. Finally, you realize that you can't go back to sleep, so you stumble into the kitchen and reach for your coffee cup.

Outside, on the back porch, where you always take your morning coffee, you rub your eyes and light your first cigarette.

The phone rings. It's much too early for anybody to be calling, you think, as you walk to the phone.

It's your mother.

"Turn on CNN," she says. "There's been a terrible terrorist attack."

You mumble your assent, and she tells you that this is really important, something you can't ignore.

"Okay," you say, "I'll turn it on."

Not understanding the gravity of the situation, you go back to your coffee on the porch. Your neighbor from the apartment below is outside, and she asks you if you've heard the news.

"The World Trade Center is gone," she says. "They've completely destroyed it."

Still you stubbornly continue your coffee/cigarettes wake up routine. You even shower and check your e-mail before you turn on the television.

Your first reaction to seeing the CNN reporters talk about the events of September 11, 2001, is a numbing sense of shock. All of a sudden, all of your petty grievances with life fade away, and the normal daily routines are completely suspended. You even feel a little guilty, which you recall is a normal response to seeing the innocent suffer through no fault of their own.

The next several days are spent in front of the television as every moment brings another shudder of fear, another brick in a wall of dread.

At some point, your father calls, angry and upset.

"We should nuke them immediately," he says.

Being a retired Army officer, he is completely outraged by the attack on the Pentagon. He pities the military people who died that day, and he is nearly in tears when he talks about it.

He asks you for your reaction, and you realize suddenly that you don't know what to say. All your confusion and fear seems to block out any meaningful response. The numbness continues.

"You should talk about it," he says. "It will make you feel better."

You mumble something lame about wishing the cleanup and the identification of bodies would go faster. Your father talks a little more, then he rings off to go back to the television.

That first Friday after the attack you go to your brother's house for dinner.

He has a gift for you, a promotional poster for Bob Dylan's latest CD, *Love And Theft*. The poster says that the album will be in stores on Tuesday, September 11. Your brother makes mention of the release date, and you both shake your heads.

You thank your brother for the poster, and later you hang it on the wall.

OSAMA BIN LADEN AND THE VISIONS

A few months later, in mid-December 2001, the famous videotape of Osama Bin Laden meeting with fellow terrorists in Afghanistan is released to the public. Bin Laden himself speaks very little on the tape, but he does give an account of some of the planning involved in the attacks.

"The brothers, who conducted the operation," Bin Laden said, "all they knew was that they have a martyrdom operation, and we asked each of them to go to America. But they didn't know anything about the operation, not even one letter. But they were trained and we did not reveal the operation to them until they are there and just before they boarded the planes."

Bin Laden goes on to say that the operatives trained to fly did not know each other and that strict secrecy was maintained during the planning stages.

Someone in the crowd asks Bin Laden to tell the group about a dream of one of their members named Abu-Da'ud.

Bin Laden obliges him.

"We were at a camp of one of the brother's guards," he begins, "in Qandahar. This brother belonged to the majority of the group. He came close and told me that he saw, in a dream, a tall building in America, and in the same dream he saw Mukhtar teaching them how to play karate. At that point, I was worried that maybe the secret would be revealed if everyone starts seeing it in their dream. So I closed the subject. I told him if he sees another dream, not to tell anybody, because people will be upset with him."

One can only wonder at the reason for this prophetic dream, which was apparently so accurate that Bin Laden felt the need to suppress any reporting of the dream lest it interfere with the diabolical plans already laid out.

THE PROPHETIC DREAMS OF THE HENCHMEN

The videotape gives an excellent education in some of what goes on in the shadowy realm of Arab terrorism. Nearly every sentence that is uttered is peppered with phrases like "Allah be praised" or "Thanks be to Allah." It reminds one of the cold, mechanistic world of George Orwell's monumental novel about totalitarianism, 1984, where the slightest deviation from Big Brother's party line can lead to imprisonment or worse.

It is that same blind allegiance to the goals set by the terrorist leadership that most likely prompts the stories of dreams and visions that come up in the conversation on the videotape. Surely, they think, no one can doubt their loyalty if Allah has sent them a dream!

One of the visions Bin Laden talks about begins after an inaudible section of the tape.

"He told me a year ago: 'I saw in a dream, we were playing a soccer game against the Americans. When our team showed up in the field, they were all pilots!' He said: 'So I wondered if that was a soccer game or a pilot game? Our players were pilots.' He (Abu-Al-Hasan) didn't know anything about the operation until he heard it on the radio. He said the game went on and we defeated them. That was a good omen for us."

Moments later, a person named "Shaykh" tells the story of other dreams and visions.

"One of the good religious people," Shaykh says, "has left everything and come here. He told me, 'I saw a vision. I was in a huge plane, long and wide. I was carrying it on my shoulders and I walked from the road to the desert for a half a kilometer. I was dragging the plane.' I listened to him and I prayed to Allah to help him. Another person told me that last year he saw, but I didn't understand and I told him I don't understand. He said, 'I saw people who left for jihad . . . and they found themselves in New York . . . . in Washington and New York.' I said, 'What is this?' He told me the plane hit the building. That was last year. We haven't thought much about it. But, when the incidents happened he came to me and said, 'Did you see this . . . . this is strange.'

"I have another man . . . . my God . . . . he said and swore by Allah that his wife had seen the incident a week earlier. She saw the plane crashing into a building . . . . that was unbelievable, my God."

The terrorists seem shaken by the series of predictive dreams and visions, as though they recognize that the power that sent them is fearful indeed. One wonders if they simply made most of them up in order to display a fervent loyalty to the Islamic cause, which again is so repressive that no one dares be seen to stand outside the limited confines of the faith.

YOUR OWN PROPHETIC DREAMS

You couldn't really tell yourself that you had known what was coming, but neither could you deny what you had dreamed. It was a recurring dream, one that you dreamed many times over a period of months, maybe even years.

You were standing near the runway of Los Angeles International Airport with some members of your family, awaiting the arrival of a flight bearing one of your loved ones. You glanced up and there was a plane seeming to hover in midair before it simply crashed to the ground in front of you. Somehow, like it was being beamed into your heard, there was a sickening realization that the pilot flying the plane had wanted to die, that he was committing suicide by simply letting the plane fall from the sky.

A long time passed, and you dreamed the dream fairly frequently, with many small variations. But always the same shock of seeing the pilot's suicide would wake you from your nightmare.

When the Egyptian Flight 300 incident happened, it was briefly kicked around that perhaps that pilot had been a suicide, since on the cockpit tape recording you hear him praying to Allah for the salvation of his soul. The prayer was dismissed by others, however, who said the prayer was the perfectly natural response of a Moslem who knew he was going to die and did not imply suicide in any way.

Still you felt that perhaps your dream had been answered and that was that. But the dream continued, sometimes frequently, sometimes rarely and always only fleetingly. When the September 11 events happened, you knew the dream had finally been literally answered, and you began to wonder, dreadfully, if you still had other dreams ahead of you.

THE PROPHETS FULFILLED?

In the first days following the attack, people were already arguing that the events were the fulfillment of prophecy, both in the Bible and in the work of Nostradamus. While the prophecies of course strengthened the idea that something close to the End of the World was happening, they also provided a kind of reassurance that such terrible events are not left to chance, or to the whims of a few madmen with a lust for death.

Isaiah 30:25 was one prophecy quoted at the time. It reads, "And upon every lofty mountain and every high hill there will be brooks running with water, in the day of the great slaughter, when the towers fall."

While it's a little difficult to decode the reference to running water, unless it means something like "Cry me a river," the more relevant part that reads, "in the day of the great slaughter, when the towers fall," seems to match the September 11 events to an unsettlingly uncanny degree. Further on in Isaiah 30, the Lord promises to heal the wounds of his people while swearing vengeance on the enemies of Israel.

It is a widely held belief that one of the motivating reasons for the terrorist attack was that America persists in being an ally to Israel, and is in fact one of the few real allies that Israel has. Perhaps we were intended to be so threatened by acts of terrorism within our own borders that we would simply turn coward and desert Israel in its time of need. Who knows?

Nostradamus also made a couple of predictions that were said to have been fulfilled by the attacks. An analysis of those pertinent quatrains will appear in a later part of this book.

IS IT THE END OF TIME?

It's been a while since the September 11 attacks, and you still haven't been able to assimilate what has happened. There was a time when you felt that the prophets would be fulfilled quickly, and with, to use an expression, a real vengeance. Now the days drag on again, and the country is on the road to recovery, proudly displaying flags and holding their heads high in the face of the enemy.

Is it, as Winston Churchill might have said were he here to see this, not the beginning of the end, but instead the end of the beginning? Have we crossed over into some time zone where the ticking of the clock that presides over the Last Days has commenced to count down, announcing finally the horrifying chain of events that will culminate in Armageddon and find release in the Second Coming of Jesus Christ?

If you had those answers, you tell yourself, there would be no need to write this book, then, would there?

These pictures were taken over Kikar Hamedina in Tel Aviv.

At 30.9.92 Udi and Smadar Baraban took the pictures of 3 Glowing objects over "Kikar Hamedina" at Tel Aviv for 30 minutes.
4 years after the couple claims they were visited by grey aliens.
with silvery rays in their eyes.
Smadar claims :" they paralized me and sucked out info."

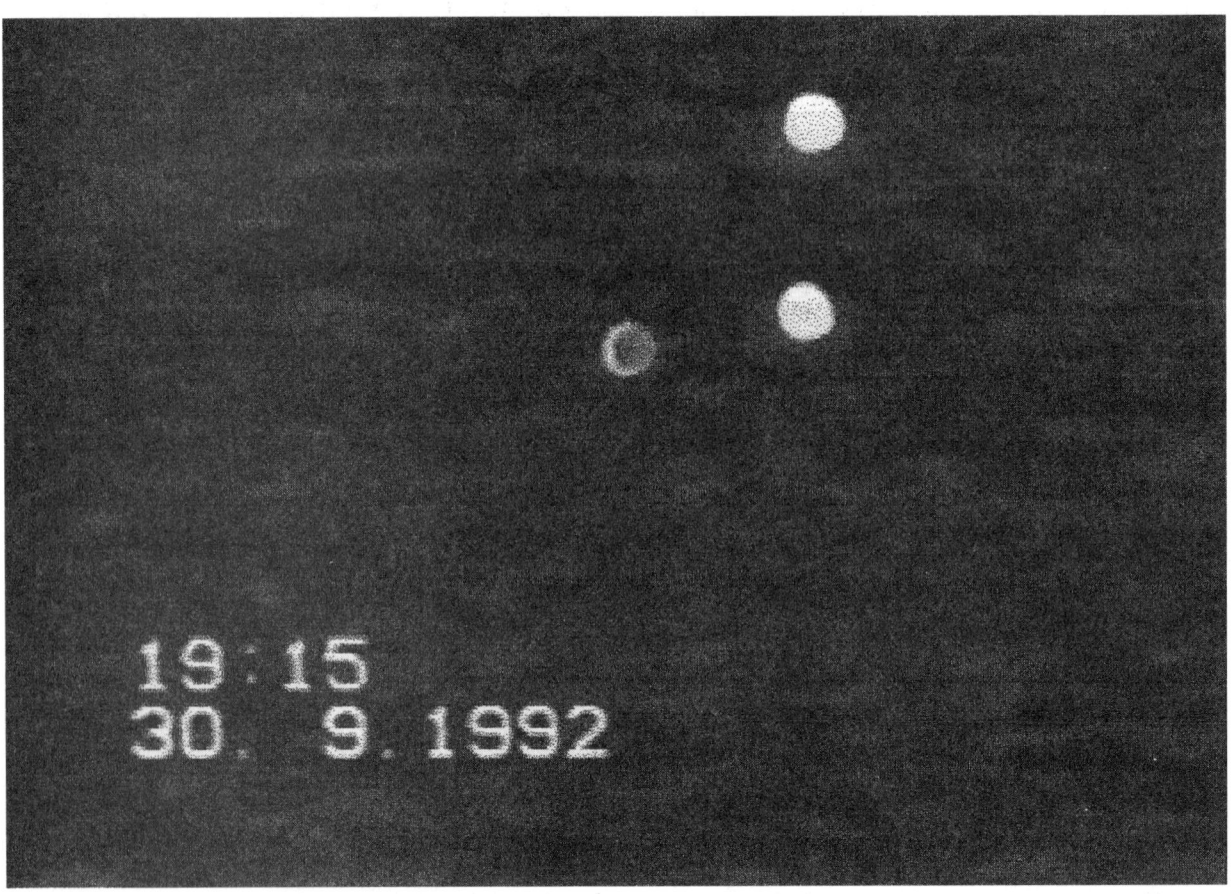

Chapter Two
The Aliens In Scripture

- *Does the Old Testament contain an ancient Hebrew name for God that implies He is really a plural entity, a gathering of "gods" organized along lines similar to what we now know of the aliens?*
- *Did the prophet Ezekiel encounter a UFO, and was he even abducted by aliens in much the same manner as modern abductees?*
- *Was Jesus Christ's ascension into heaven in full view of his disciples merely another instance of a human being brought aboard a UFO, waiting in the sky, by teleportation?*
- *Do some key verses in the Book of Isaiah point to the alien genetic hybridization program as being an evolutionary method of change being used by the God of the Bible?*
- *Was Jesus really an alien, a typical "gray" who changed his form to fit a given situation?*

The Bible has been called the world's greatest book of UFOlogy by some and dismissed as totally unrelated in any conclusive way to the modern UFO phenomenon at all by others. It becomes a matter of totally subjective faith as both sides argue their case without the slightest bit of empirical proof or totally convincing scientific evidence. Belief in the Bible and in the UFO phenomenon itself are both a matter of a preference based on the inner mind's personal perceptions and the heart's emotional need for conclusions it can be comfortable with.

My own belief is that both the Bible and the UFO phenomenon are inseparably related and represent a form of divine revelation from the Heavenly Ones On High who themselves determine the moment they make the truth of their existence and presence known to the world in general. An unplanned, seemingly accidental "discovery" of the truth is not possible without them. There is no proof of God in the most objective terms unless he himself makes that truth evident through his own divine revelation of himself. Seeing is believing, but only when God is ready for us to see.

THE HEAVENLY ONES

Most people's understanding of the God of the Bible involves a monotheistic belief in one God, usually depicted as a gray-bearded Father whose commanding presence oversees not only mankind but the entire universe as well. Everything is in subordination to the Ancient of Days, as the Book of Daniel calls him.

The reader may be surprised to learn that there are other versions of God contained in the Bible. The ancient Hebrew word "Elohim," one of the most frequently used names for God throughout the Old Testament, actually translates more closely to "the gods" than to a simple monotheistic name for One God. It includes not only a multiple reference to more than one God, but can even be used to denote mere mortals of high rank, such as judges or prophets.

One relatively easy way to see this plural reference to "the gods" comes from the Book of Genesis, 3:22-24. After meting out his punishments to Adam, Eve and the serpent, God says, '"Behold, the man has become like one of us, knowing good and evil; and now, lest he put forth his hand and take also of the tree of life, and eat, and live forever,' therefore the Lord God sent him forth from the Garden of Eden, to till the ground from which he was taken. He drove out the man; and at the east of the Garden of Eden he placed the cherubim, and a flaming sword which turned every way, to guard the way of the tree of life."

When God says "the man has become like one of us," to whom is he addressing that statement? Who are these friends he apparently counts as equals, or something close to being equal? Are we to assume that his angelic servants are on such an even level with him? What about the reference to a cherubim later in the passage? Is the angel sent to guard the tree of life one of those God refers to as knowing good and evil and existing on an apparently even keel with him?

The obvious inference is that God presides over a council of equals or near equals who are also technically called "God" by virtue of the term "Elohim."

There is another verse from Genesis that has similar implications. In Genesis 1: 26-27, the scripture says, "Then God said, 'Let us make man in our image, after our likeness; and let them have dominion over the fish of the sea, and over the birds of the air, and over the cattle, and over all the earth.' So God created man in his own image, in the image of God he created him, male and female he created them."

Again, God addresses his remarks to an unseen group offstage, with the language implying that God is a plural entity, made "in our image," and again both "male and female." The aliens reported in countless abduction accounts are nearly always decidedly either male or female, and their working together in harmony is a wonder to behold.

Still another way the various levels of "gods" are grouped is illustrated by a pair of verses from the Book of Job, 33:23-24, "If there be for him an angel, a mediator, one

There exists a council of angels, a thousand to be exact, that work to mediate between God and man and make intercession for the righteous when they are judged.

of the thousand, to declare to man what is right for him, and he is gracious to him, and says, 'Deliver him from going down into the Pit, I have found a ransom . . . "

The verse implies that there exists a council of angels, a thousand to be exact, that work to mediate between God and man and make intercession for the righteous when they are judged. The picture that begins to emerge is one of a well-organized hierarchy of heavenly beings with God at the top and with varying ranks of gods and angels below who have a kind of workaday relationship with one another as they supervise the affairs of men.

How perfectly such a system overlays with what we know about the aliens as witnessed to by the experiences of many abductees, from the Barney and Betty Hill case of the early 1960s up through the most recent abduction accounts of the New Millennium! But there will be more discussion about that later. Let's continue to explore the ways aliens figure in scripture.

THE FAMOUS WHIRLING WHEELS OF EZEKIEL

The words written by the Prophet Ezekiel are perhaps the most widely known section of the Bible to be interpreted as having to do with our modern day perception of UFOs. Beginning in the mid-1960s, everyone from author and researcher Erich Von Daniken to NASA scientist Josef F. Blumrich argued quite convincingly that what Ezekiel describes in his account of his meeting with God is in fact the landing of a UFO.

Beginning with Ezekiel 1:4-10, the prophet's account reads, "As I looked, behold, a stormy wind came out of the north, and a great cloud, with brightness round about it, and fire flashing forth continually, and in the midst of the fire, as it were gleaming bronze. And from the midst of it came the likeness of four living creatures. And this was their appearance: they had the form of men, but each had four faces, and each of them had four wings. Their legs were straight, and the soles of their feet were like the sole of a calf's foot; and they sparkled like burnished bronze. Under their wings on their four sides they had human hands. And the four had their faces and their wings thus: their wings touched one another; they went every one straight forward, without turning as they went. As for the likeness of their faces, each had the face of a man in front; the four had the face of a lion on the right side, the four had the face of an ox on the left side, and the four had the face of an eagle at the back."

Ezekiel Chap. 1. Ver. 1. to 28.

EZEKIEL'S VISION

"As I looked, behold, a stormy wind came out of the north, and a great cloud, with brightness round about it, and fire flashing forth continually, and in the midst of the fire, as it were gleaming bronze."

The sudden appearance of a UFO in our time might look much the same! A great cloud, with a brightness round about it, and fire flashing forth continually—doesn't that closely resemble the frequently sighted form of a UFO with its flashing lights and overwhelming otherworldly presence? The four living creatures that Ezekiel describes as looking like human beings, but with the additional animal characteristics, may be an early attempt to report the appearance of aliens from within the craft—human looking, but with certain important differences.

Again, bright lights are alluded to beginning in verse 13: "In the midst of the living creatures there was something that looked like burning coals of fire, like torches moving to and fro among the living creatures; and the fire was bright, and out of the fire went forth lightning. And the living creatures darted to and fro, like a flash of lightning."

Later, in Ezekiel Chapter 10:9, and following, the ancient prophet's testimony reads, "And I looked, and behold, there were four wheels beside the cherubim, one beside each cherub; and the appearance of the wheels was like sparkling chrysolite. And as for their appearance, the four had the same likeness, as if a wheel within a wheel . . . And their rims, and their spokes, and the wheels were full of eyes round about—the wheels that the four of them had. As for the wheels, they were called in my hearing the whirling wheels . . . . Then the glory of the Lord went forth from the threshold of the house and stood over the cherubim. And the cherubim lifted up their wings and mounted up from the earth in my sight as they went forth, with the wheels beside them; and they stood at the door of the east gate of the house of the Lord; and the glory of the God of Israel was over them. Those were the living creatures that I saw underneath the God of Israel by the river Chebar; and I knew that they were cherubim. Each had four faces, and each four wings, and underneath their wings the semblance of human hands. And as for the likeness of their faces, they were the very faces whose appearance I had seen by the river Chebar. They went every one straight forward."

Immediately, many obvious correlations spring to mind. The description of a "wheel within a wheel" is easily seen to be an ancient attempt to express the movement of a disc-shaped craft, with a sparkling, shiny metallic construction. The wheels being "full of eyes round about" could be a reference to portholes, or small circular windows, which are another familiar detail of modern day UFO sightings accounts.

Backtracking to Ezekiel 3:14-15, the prophet is even abducted for a brief period: "The Spirit lifted me up and took me away, and I went in bitterness in the heat of my spirit, the hand of the Lord being strong upon me: and I came to the exiles at Telabib, who dwelt by the river Chebar. And I sat there overwhelmed among them seven days."

This is an excellent description of the disorientation and trauma often experienced by modern day abductees, "in bitterness in the heat of my spirit," and the strange sense of aftermath that lingers on after the abductee has been returned, as the prophet sits "overwhelmed" for seven days.

THE MIRACLES ARE FOR REAL

The Bible is a book full of miracles and wonders. But for unbelievers, it is exactly those miracles that make faith in the Bible a non-issue. Science is based on logic and repeatable experiments. How can they believe in a God whose very existence is dependent on things they "know" to be impossible?

To argue the contrary position, however, many of the miracles reported in both the Old and New Testament have been not only duplicated by modern day UFOs and their alien occupants, but are even quite commonplace occurrences in the current literature on sightings and abductions.

For instance, there is the ascension of Jesus Christ into Heaven after he appears to the disciples in order to prove to them the literal reality of his physical resurrection from the dead. This act is what gives the Christian religion its power. The same thing frequently happens at the beginning of an abduction experience when a person is physically levitated through the bedroom wall and up into a waiting ship in the skies above their home.

The aliens' genetic experiments are another example of the miraculous being commonplace. The woman with the pseudonym "Kathie Davis," whose case history forms the bulk of abduction researcher Budd Hopkins' landmark book *Intruders: The Incredible Visitations At Copley Woods* (1987), reports that, as a teenager, a doctor declared her to be pregnant. The problem was, however, that she was still a virgin! Though she wasn't able to convince anyone of her innocence, fortunately the fetus disappeared after she entered her third month, which is common with alien-induced pregnancies.

But of course the belief that the Virgin Mary really did conceive a child by the hand of God is made much more plausible by the fact that we see it happening in our time as well.

17

PROPHECIES OF THE HYBRID BABIES

The genetic experiments conducted by the aliens to create the hybrid race of half human, half alien children are one of the more commonly recurring events in the standard abduction scenario. One would think that such a phenomenon, with its heavy science fiction overtones, would be completely out of the scope of the Biblical prophets. But let's take a look at Isaiah 45: 9-11.

"Woe to him who strives with his Maker, an earthen vessel with the potter. Does the clay say to him who fashions it, 'What are you making?' or 'Your work has no handles.' Woe to him who says to a father, 'What are you begetting?' or to a woman, 'With what are you in travail?' Thus says the Lord, the Holy One of Israel, and his Maker, 'Will you question me about my children, or command me concerning the work of my hands?'"

Here it seems the Lord is trying to answer his critics while at the same time confessing to his own hand in the creation process. One can almost see the average UFO researcher leading a witness through the process of hypnotic regression and, when the subject of the hybrid babies comes up, asking questions like "What are you begetting?" or "With what are you in travail?"

One should also recall that one aspect of the alien hybridization often involves a presentation of the mutant baby to both fathers and mothers who may indeed be equally confused as well as to what they had a hand in parenting.

Returning to Isaiah, the prophet has God declaring himself to be strange and "alien" as well. Isaiah 28: 21 reads, "For the Lord will rise up as on Mount Perazin, he will be wroth as in the Valley of Gibeon, to do his deed—strange is his deed! And to work his work—alien is his work!"

Admittedly, "alien" is generally understood to be synonymous with "foreigner" and "stranger," but is it so difficult to imagine these words were written with a future context in mind? It is not hard to see that the books the prophets wrote are intended to serve as a time capsule-type message to the future world, our present world, in which the word "alien" read as "extraterrestrial" was a very much intended pun.

Isaiah 42: 9 reads, "Behold the former things have come to pass, and new things I now declare; before they spring forth I tell you of them." It is followed shortly by Isaiah 43: 18-19, which reads, "Remember not the former things, nor consider the things of old. Behold, I am doing a new thing; now it springs forth, do you not perceive it?"

Both of these passages portray the Lord as doing something new under the sun, showing mankind an aspect of creation not yet seen yet still the bona fide creation of the Lord of Israel. Perhaps, without reading an understanding in where it does not belong (though anyone attempting this argument would fall prey to that), these verses can also have been referring to an intended evolutionary change from Homo Sapiens to whatever the hybrid children are ultimately called.

When you connect the preceding verses, the Lord declares himself to be an alien carrying out an alien act, that is something new and not previously understood, involving the begetting and birth of children that he is loathe to see suffer criticism. Does that not fit rather neatly the patterns of abduction and the mutant children these experiences many times involve, as well as the aliens' obvious concern for and pride in these hybrid children?

As abduction researcher David Jacobs wrote in *Secret Life* (1992), the aliens often say to their reluctant human parent subjects, "This is a good baby! What a good baby!" The God of the Bible seems to have little tolerance for those slow to see his unfolding plan, even if it involves babies that can truthfully be called "mutations."

WAS JESUS AN ALIEN?

There exists quite a large body of written work that was intended to be viewed as inspired scripture but was disavowed by the church fathers as being unworthy to be included in the canon of "acceptable" books of the Bible. One example is "The Acts of John," which claimed to have been written by the same person as "The Gospel of John" in the New Testament, and contains elements of both Gnostic and orthodox beliefs. "The Acts of John" was read aloud in part at the Council of Nicaea, where the decisions about what was worthy of inclusion in the New Testament were made, and was formally condemned.

The late great scholar of myth, Joseph Campbell, quotes a large section of the apocryphal book in *Occidental Mythology, The Masks of God*. Here is how Campbell sets the scene:

"In the 'Acts of John' we find the following astonishing rendition of the scene of Christ's summoning of his apostles at the Sea of Galilee. The Messiah has just come from his desert fast of forty days and his victory there over Satan. John and James are in their boat, fishing. Christ appears on the shore. And John is supposed to be telling, now, of the occasion."

What follows is directly from the "Acts of John," and it is astonishing indeed.

"For when he had chosen Peter and Andrew, who were brothers, he came to me and James my brother, saying, 'I have need of you, come unto me.' And my brother, hearing that, said to me, 'John, what does that child want who is on the shore there and called to us?' And I said, 'What child?' And he said again, 'The one beckoning to us.' And I answered: 'Because of the long watch we have kept at sea, you are not seeing right, my brother James. But do you not see the man who is standing there, comely, fair, and of cheerful countenance?' But he answered, 'Him, brother, I do not see. But let us go, and we shall see what he wants.'"Already the two brothers are in disagreement. James sees a child beckoning, while John sees a full grown adult. The passage continues.

"And so, when we had brought our boat to land, we saw him, also, helping us to settle it; and when we had left, thinking to follow him, he appeared to me to be rather bald, but with a beard thick and flowing, but to James he seemed a youth whose beard had newly come. We were therefore, both of us, perplexed as to what we had seen should mean."

This seems to really hit the nail on its head. To John, Jesus appears to be bald! One wonders if he is seeing a gray alien morphing between his own normally bald physical makeup and something more human, hence the appearance of a thick beard at other moments. Again, the passage goes on.

"And as we followed him, continuing, we both were, little by little, even more perplexed as we considered the matter. For in my case there appeared this still more wonderful thing: I would try to watch him secretly, and I never at any time saw his eyes blinking, but only open. And often he would appear to me to be a little man, uncomely, but then again as one reaching up to heaven. Moreover, there was in him another marvel: when we sat to eat he would clasp me to his breast, and sometimes the breast felt to me to be smooth and tender, but sometimes hard like stone . . ."

The report of Christ's eyes never blinking suggests that perhaps John is seeing the large, black eyes of a gray alien, which many witnesses report as giving off an unblinking stare as they scan the abductee's mind, perhaps for the purpose of analyzing his emotions.

"Another glory," John continues, "also, would I tell you, my brethren: namely, that sometimes when I would take hold of him, I would meet with a material and solid body, but again, at other times, when I touched him, the substance was immaterial, and as if it existed not at all. And if at any time he were invited by some Pharisee and accepted the invitation, we accompanied him; and there was set before each of us a loaf by those who entertained; and with us, he too received one. But his own he would bless and apportion among us. And of that little, every one was filled, and our own loaves were saved whole, so that those who had invited him were amazed. And often when I walked with him, I desired to see the print of his foot, whether it appeared on the earth; for I saw him, as it were, sustaining himself above the earth: and I never saw it."

Again, wonders upon wonders. Christ's body is reported to hover at times between the material and the immaterial. His feet apparently don't touch the ground, and thus he leaves no footprints behind him. Both of these miracles are common elements of the aliens as recounted in abduction stories. They reportedly change form and disappear at will, and are sometimes said to hover inches above the ground and simply float from place to place. What is said of the aliens was also said of Christ two thousand years ago.

"And these things I tell you, my brethren," John concludes, "for the encouragement of your faith in him; for we must, at present, keep silence concerning his mighty and wonderful works, in as much as they are unspeakable and, it may be, cannot at all be uttered or be heard."

This last indicates a similar need to keep silent about an extraordinary experience that many abductees share with John. The reluctance to speak openly about something so strange springs primarily from the witness's fear that they will not be believed, or that they will be called crazy for relating a story so bizarre without having the means to "prove" that the events really happened.

There are many other passages in the Bible that would serve to demonstrate a relationship between the gods and angels of ancient times and the aliens of our own time. Hopefully this chapter has made that relationship sufficiently palpable to the reader.

Chapter Three
Good And Evil Among The Abductees

"I was given a vision of 'humanity,'" Katharina Wilson states. "'Humanity' was standing in line inside a mall at a burger joint, content with their minimum wage jobs. They weren't striving for anything more in life. They weren't trying to educate themselves. They weren't trying to make a positive difference. They were satisfied. A short, pudgy female Being with dark skin and funny looking glasses was standing next to me. She was telepathically tuning into my thoughts and feelings. I said to her, 'I can't believe they're satisfied with this. Eating animals and existing to work . . . . it's unacceptable.'" The female telepathically replied, matter-of-factly. 'They are receptacles.'"

"I sat with my legs partly bent and my hands in my lap. Although I cannot recall this in any detail, I may have been leaning against something. I was still absent sensation. Across the depression to my left there was a small individual whom I could see only out of the corner of my eye. This person was wearing a gray-tan body suit and sitting on the ground with knees drawn up and hands clasped around them. There were two dark eyeholes and a round mouth hole. I had the impression of a facemask.

"I felt that I was under the exact and detailed control of whomever had me. I could not move my head, or my hands, or any part of my body save my eyes . . . . Immediately on my right was another figure, this one invisible except for an occasional flash of movement. This person was working busily at something that seemed to have to do with the right side of my head. It wore dark-blue overalls and was extremely fast.

"The next thing I knew, I was sitting in a messy round room . . . . The fear was so powerful that it seemed to make my personality completely evaporate. This was not a theoretical or even a mental experience, but something profoundly physical . . . . I was so scared that my memories are indistinct and covered by amnesia. Even as I write this, I am aware that a great deal more happened. I just can't get to it."
--Whitley Streiber, *Communion, A True Story*, 1987

"Suddenly, the electric lights began to flicker hesitantly and then blinked out, throwing the house into darkness and confusion and sending frightened children scurrying into the kitchen to find their mother. Almost at the same time, the family saw a curious pink light shining through the kitchen window. Ten years later, under hypnosis, Betty and Becky Andreasson would describe the scene as follows:

Betty: Suddenly the lights were off, and we wondered, what was it? And we looked over and there was a . . . by the window, the small kitchen window . . . I can see like a light, sort of pink right now. And now the light is getting brighter. It's reddish-orange, and it's pulsating. I said to the children, 'Be quiet, and quick, get in the living room, and whatever it is will go away.' It seemed like the whole house had a vacuum over it. Like stillness all around, like stillness.

Becky: The next thing I knew, Mom was going, 'Shhh! Be quiet!' There's some huge pulsating glow that was out in the kitchen. It was outside. Like a big glow!

"When the bright light first flashed through the kitchen window, Becky had returned into the living room in response to her mother's commands. Looking down the hallway into the kitchen, she noticed a dark silhouetted shape bobbing in front of the light source shining through the kitchen window. Then, everything went black. At that same moment, Becky, her grandfather, and all family members except Betty found themselves unable to move, unaware of anything else.

Betty: There's some . . . the lights are back on now and, ah, there are beings standing there and they're talking with me, but not with their mouths. They've got big heads. They came through the door. They came in like follow-the-leader. They are starting to come through the door now. Right through the wood, one right after the other. It's amazing. Coming through. And I stood back a little. Was it real? And they are coming, one after another . . . Now they are all inside. I thought, how did they ever do that? How did they get in here like that? I'm thinking they must be angels, because Jesus was able to walk through doors and walls and walk on water. Must be angels. . . And Scriptures keep coming into my mind where it says, 'Entertain the stranger, for it may be angels unaware.'"

--Raymond Fowler, *The Andreasson Affair*, 1979

"There was an oval-shaped object hovering over the top of the apartment building two or three blocks up from where we were sitting. We didn't know where it came from, it happened too fast. Its lights turned from a bright reddish-orange to a whitish-blue coming out of the bottom of it. There on the side of the craft near the top of it, just above the protruding saucer ledge, I could see horizontal, rectangular-shaped windows around the object. At the very edge of the object, on the edge of the protruding saucer ledge, were green rotating lights rotating round and round while the craft stood still, just hovering off of the building. It moved out away from the building and lowered itself to the apartment window below, about two windows down. I yelled for my partner sitting behind the wheel of the car. He was astonished as I was. Yes, it was like science fiction objects that we used to laugh at many years ago on TV . . . .

"We wanted to get out of the car to see what we could do. What were we going to do? Shoot at it? We stayed in the car and the worst happened. A little girl or woman wearing a full white gown sailed out of the window in a fetal position. Linda was there now in a standing position in midair in this beam of light. She looked like an angel or a Christmas tree doll. Then the lights underneath the object dimmed and we directed ourselves toward Linda.

"With my binoculars I could see three of the ugliest creatures I ever saw. I don't know what they were. They weren't human. Their heads were all out of proportion. Very large heads with no hair. The eyes were very large, very large eyes. I don't know what color they were, maybe white. Very thin, too thin, smaller than Linda in height. One of them was standing above her in midair and two were beneath her. Those buggers were escorting her into the craft. They were completely in charge, all right . . . . She was gone, they took her away." [A partial transcript of a recording made by "Richard," the pseudonym of a security guard who was one of the eyewitnesses to Linda Cortile's abduction in November of 1989.]
    --Budd Hopkins, *Witnessed*: *The True Story of the Brooklyn Bridge Abductions*, 1996

According to Dr. John Mack, Harvard psychiatrist and author of two essential books on abduction, ***Abduction*** (1994) and ***Passport To The Cosmos*** (1999), one of the most common reactions a person has to becoming aware of their abduction experiences is something he labeled "ontological shock." The sudden jolt to the system of learning there is another reality never before dreamed of by the abductee causes a dramatic shift in consciousness, and an entirely new realm of experience must be assimilated.

That assimilation process, however, is often slow and tortuous. And among the many subjects the abductee is forced to think differently about, religion stands out as one of the major problem areas. An abductee must often ask, "How did God let this happen to me?" or any of a number of theological and philosophical questions that bombard the mind as the person begins to try to navigate between the abduction experience and what was once "normal" reality.

When I began to take an interest in the UFO phenomenon, as a Christian and a journalist, the thing I was most curious about was the moral quality of the aliens, whether we were dealing with proverbial soul-stealing demons or soul-healing angels in the increasingly numerous accounts of sightings and abductions. The answers I got were as vague and as inconclusive as the answers to most of the other aspects of the phenomenon. Like every other "unknown," the moral nature of the UFO occupants was open to any number of contradictory and unsatisfying conclusions.

Beginning in the spring of 1989, I interviewed some of the famous researchers and witnesses, such as Raymond Fowler, Budd Hopkins, Betty Andreasson Luca and Whitley Strieber, among many others. In each case, at some point, I asked for their moral and religious perspectives on their research and experiences. The interviewees responded with a wide range of moral responses, running the gamut from reluctant agnosticism to heartfelt belief in the righteousness of the abducting aliens.

RAYMOND FOWLER

Raymond Fowler is a veteran UFO researcher and the author of numerous books on the subject of alien abduction. He served with the US Air Force as a Security Officer and spent twenty-five years with GTE Government Systems where he worked as Task Manager and Senior Planner for several major weapons systems, including the Minuteman and MX missiles. As a director of investigations for the Mutual UFO Network, he appeared frequently on such television programs as Good Morning America, Unsolved Mysteries, and Sightings.

Fowler is perhaps best known for his five-part series on abductee Betty Andreasson Luca, which began in 1979 with *The Andreasson Affair*, and was followed by *The Andreasson Affair Phase Two* (1982), *The Watchers* (1990), *The Watchers II* (1995) and *The Andreasson Legacy* (1997).

In an interview I conducted with Fowler in 1991, he said, "I started officially investigating the UFO phenomenon in 1963. I have now found that the phenomenon has been investigating me since 1938!"

Fowler's discovery that he was also an abductee was first revealed in *The Watchers*, which was the above mentioned third installment of the complex research into Betty Andreasson Luca and her long history of contact with extraterrestrials. Being on both sides of the subject, as a researcher and an experiencer, gives Fowler a uniquely well-informed perspective on the subject.

I asked Fowler the following: You and Betty are both Christians who feel these experiences have a religious overtone. Do prophecies of the Apocalypse enter your thinking about the aliens? Do you think the world, as we know it today, is doomed by the things the aliens are said to warn us against, like nuclear war or ecological disaster?

"Betty certainly believes," Fowler began, "that her experiences are angelic in nature, and that they correspond to her Christian belief system, which would include prophecies of the Apocalypse and the Second Coming of Christ. As Christians, both of us believe that Jesus Christ is our only hope. I would like to believe that such a connection exists and that past and present UFO manifestations in our history have a direct connection with the Judeo-Christian tradition. However, all one can really say for sure is that what is being seen today was also seen in Biblical times, only it would have been interpreted within a religious context, not a scientific one. Conversely, if some of the phenomena reported in Biblical accounts were reported today, they would be placed in a UFO context."

FOWLER'S CHRISTIAN STRUGGLE

In another interview I did with Fowler in 1997, he spoke movingly about his struggle to balance his abduction experiences with his Christian beliefs.

"On the objective side of my faith," he said, "there has been an ever-growing tension between my theological beliefs and my theoretical hypotheses about the origin and meaning behind the UFO phenomenon and my own apparent abductions. My former pastor, whose wife had a Close Encounter experience of the First Kind [sighting a ship], once asked me how I integrated my UFO research and experiences with my Christian faith. I replied that at the present time I had no choice but to 'compartmentalize' them.

"In short," he continued, "I find myself living a double life as a UFO researcher/experiencer on the one hand and a devoted Christian on the other while trying to erect a harmonious bridge between the two. Thus I find myself living with a continual tension between two worlds, both of which are very real to me."

Fowler told the story of how he had experienced an emotion he called "Unconditional Love" in both a Christian context and an alien one, and that they seemed to be related—at least coincidentally. The story began when Fowler was still in adolescence.

"It was on the evening of May 19, 1950," he said. "Several weeks earlier, I had befriended a boy from a broken home who was going to be placed in a state institution for the homeless. I had persuaded my parents to let him live with us. He shared my room. He and his friends were Christians, and over those weeks they shared their faith with me.

"On the night in question," he went on, "unknown to my roommate at the time, while lying in bed, I privately received Christ into my life. When doing so, I experienced an inner feeling of pure, unconditional love as an outside Presence entered and filled my being. As this was happening to me, my roommate exclaimed that there was a bright light hovering over the house. But I paid little attention to what he said because of what was happening to me experientially. It was only years later, when he visited me again and again told me about the bright light that we both wondered if it was UFO-related. A check of astronomical records revealed no such bright object in the sky on that date and time."

That sensation of unconditional love has happened to Fowler on more than one occasion.

"I have felt this identical feeling of unconditional love," he said, "envelop me on a number of occasions, including during what seem to have been UFO abductions. For example, I felt it as a child when awakened by a lady enveloped in light who floated me through my bedroom window up a beam of light to some lights in the sky. So from the very beginning, and throughout my Christian walk of life, there seems to be at least a subjective, mystical-like, coincidental connection between my UFO and Christian-related experiences."

So again I asked if Fowler's UFO research and experiences had affected his religious beliefs.

"Sure they have," he said, "and hopefully, in the long run, for the good—although I am prepared to accept the bad as well. On the one hand, I continue to attend church, sing in the choir, teach adult Sunday school and attempt with God's help to live a good Christian life. On the other hand, I continue to live in tension as I attempt to construct a bridge between two sometimes seemingly opposing but true experiences—the double life of a Christian believer and UFO experiencer."

BETTY ANDREASSON LUCA

Betty Andreasson Luca was born in Fitchburg, Massachusetts, in 1937, to devoutly

Pentecostal Christian parents. She married James Andreasson, and the couple became the parents of seven children. Betty and James divorced, and she later married Bob Luca, who was also an alien abductee.

Betty's first recalled abduction experience is partially recounted at the beginning of this chapter. The events took place in the family house in South Ashburnham, Massachusetts, in 1967. It was the first of many experiences that Betty would recall only after the fact and while under hypnosis. Raymond Fowler helped lead her through her regressive hypnosis sessions and offered moral support and educated insight as well as writing the books on her continuing story mentioned earlier.

Luca, who began working with Fowler to uncover her abduction experiences more than twenty-five years ago, seems not to suffer from the same lingering doubt as Fowler or to view her contact with aliens as in some way diametrically opposed to her Christian beliefs.

I first interviewed Luca in 1991, a few months after I had spoken to Fowler. Luca was of particular interest to me because she was an abductee who unflinchingly believed she had been contacted by angels, a leap of faith many abductees were unable to make.

"I believe that UFO contacts are of an angelic nature," Luca said, "whether good or bad, and I base this statement primarily on my faith and knowledge acquired during personal encounters. Regardless of whether it is God's angels or lost, fallen angels, we humans are the battleground or territory either side wishes to gain. My encounters with benevolent beings have strengthened my faith in the reality of the seldom-seen world of the government of God. His messengers have been sent to do His will, and although I have seen and heard yet not always understood, I can rest in His promises and faith."

A few years later, when I spoke to Luca again, her faith remained much the same.

"My UFO encounters with extraterrestrials," she said, "which I still believe to be Angels or Messengers, have helped me to mature as a child of God. My Christian faith is of the utmost importance to me, and I believe it has occasionally given me access to a realm rarely seen by physical eyes. And yet this God-given rite of passage can exist for everyone, for the Creator is not a respecter of persons. His love for everyone is unconditional and encompasses all.

"I've chosen the Old and New Testament," she continued, "as my road map, and embraced with all my heart the humble being who gave his all for me. He loved us more than life. When he died on a cross and rose to his celestial abode, his child began to grow inside each believer from the seeds of his Word. His child in us increases as we decrease. After complete surrender to Christ, the beginning of wisdom grew.

"It was not long before extraterrestrial visitation began," she said. "While immersed in a benign celestial world filled with mystery, the angelic host began to reveal themselves little by little."

Such a cheerful outlook stands in marked contrast to the trauma and terror reported by most abductees. But Luca had an answer for those critical voices as well.

"I cannot express enough," she said, "the real need to be grounded in faith when exposed to the spiritual world of UFOs. For once there, you will experience what eyes have not seen and ears have not heard. For the unprepared, it can be a world of sheer terror. For when man neglects to know himself and his Maker, it leaves him open to fear."

Luca acknowledged that her views are not shared by some.

"Unfortunately," she said, "many who worship today account the angels or extraterrestrials to be evil spirits. But God is the same yesterday, today and tomorrow. As in the days of yesteryear, when He spoke to Moses, Jacob, Joseph and David, to Matthew, Mark, Luke and John, He'll speak to us today through His Son, the Spirit, and The Watchers [a term Fowler and Luca sometimes use for aliens that is taken from Old Testament scriptures], and tomorrow he will be the same God for generations to come."

For Luca, alien abduction is not something God helps her endure, it is the experience of union with God Himself.

"My faith is as strong as the Rock I stand on," she said. "And because I've experienced a deep walk and been privy to personal extraterrestrial encounters, I am blessed."

I also asked Luca the following question: Does the idea of abduction match up with the Christian idea of "Rapture" in your mind? Is it meaningful to you to think of the current activities of the aliens as having something to do with the prophecies of the Apocalypse?

"Quite possibly," Luca replied. "There is scripture to support the idea. In the Book of Luke 17: 34-36, Christ says, 'In that night, there shall be two men in one bed. One shall be taken, and the other shall be left. Two women shall be grinding together. The one shall be taken, and the other left. Two men shall be in the fields, and one shall be taken, and the other left.'

"Further evidence," she continued, "that may support the Rapture is verses 30 and

31. 'Even thus shall it be in the day when the Son of Man shall be revealed. In that day, he which shall be upon the housetop and his stuff in the house, let him not come down to take it away. And he that is in the field, let him likewise not return back.'

"Doesn't it sound familiar?" she asked. "Of course most Christians believe it will be one swoop of believers, starting first with those who are in the grave and have died in faith, and those believers that remain will be caught up in the air."

So from two Christian believers come answers that rest firmly on their bedrock of faith. I know I am not alone in being consoled by their heavenly interpretation of what could otherwise be a tremendously frightening experience with no redeeming moral value at all. It is wise to be thankful for small mercies, and perhaps the mercy implied in this understanding of the abduction experience will grow as the years go on.

WHITLEY STRIEBER

Whitley Strieber is perhaps the most famous of all the abductees who have put their experiences down on paper. His hugely successful first book on the subject, **Communion**, was number one on the bestseller lists in 1987 for several weeks. He also published many sequels, including **Transformation** (1988), **Breakthrough** (1995), **The Secret School** (1997), **The Communion Letters** (1997) and **Confirmation** (1998). Strieber's struggle to come to grips with aliens he called "The Visitors" has been arduous but rewarding, not only for himself and his family, but for millions of others who have had similar events happen in their lives.

Strieber began his career as a writer of horror fiction, and authored, among many others, the hit novels **The Wolfen** and **The Hunger**, both of which were made into successful movies. When **Communion** made its initial appearance as a bestseller, it was widely suggested that Strieber had used his skills as a horror novelist to concoct simply another scary story, and had labeled it as "true" only to boost the book's sales. For Strieber, though, it was the beginning of a new life in which his alien abduction experiences were only too real.

When I asked Strieber for his views on the moral aspects of alien abduction at our first meeting in 1989, he began by saying, "I see the Visitor experience as being very similar to experiences which have happened to many other people in the past, ranging from St. Paul's unusual experience on the road to Damascus, to the apparitions of Fatima. I can see my experiences as being in line with historical encounters of supposed spirits, demons and angels. My experiences run the full gamut of all that."

When I interviewed Strieber again, in June of 1993, he had changed his religious interpretation to a rather negative one.

"I've never encountered anything," he said, "that was pleasant or angelic in any way. It's always been very difficult and very scary and, as often as not, dangerous. I've come away from this experience convinced of one thing: if there aren't any demons out there, there might as well be because these guys are indistinguishable from demons. To see them, to look into their eyes, is to be less, forever. It hurts you, takes from you forever because then you know it really exists. And that makes you less."

At this point, I was a little discouraged myself. But Strieber managed to leave a little room for hope regarding his interpretation of his friend Betty Andreasson Luca.

"The number of us who are so spiritually superb as Betty," he said, "who can really make this encounter fly, is tiny. Most of us are down in the muck struggling with it. That's why Betty is such an inspiration to me. When I was at the depths of my depression, one of the things I did was read Betty's interviews and listen to her tapes, just to hear the sound of her voice. I would also look at drawings she sent me and it helped a lot. Betty's experiences are the thing you grab onto while you're sinking."

In fairness to Strieber, he resists launching into a black versus white moral debate.

"I don't believe," he said, "in dichotomies of black and white, good and evil. It isn't the way life works and it isn't the way this experience works. It can be a very rough experience, there's no doubt about it. It is rarely a beautiful experience, in the sentimental sense of 'sweetness and light.' It is always, however, if you wish it to be, a useful experience in terms of growth of knowledge, character and understanding. But it can be devastating, which it has been for me at times, because of its sheer power and the tremendously difficult experience of facing an enigma so volatile.

"This is the most complex experience," he continued, "that anyone has ever had. The totality of the encounter experience is incredibly complex. It is shaded with dozens of different layers of meaning. To try and make it into something black and white or to divide people according to this black and white issue of whether the so-called aliens are good or bad is to fail to even begin to see what's going on. As far as I'm concerned, the UFO community, which revolves around this black or white interpretation, literally has no idea what's going on. They haven't even begun."

I interviewed Strieber again a few years later and asked him if his experiences had affected his religious beliefs any differently since we last discussed the subject.

"There's never been much of a connection," he said. "No matter what my religious beliefs at any given time may or may not have been, the close encounter experience simply doesn't affect them. I have been many different things in my life. As a child, I was a Catholic. When I grew up, I joined the Gurdjieef Foundation [where I studied meditation] and became very interested in 'waking up' and not so interested in my Catholic background. I went through a period of being very interested in paganism. I returned to Catholicism again, and now I am sort of less interested in it. There are elements of Catholicism, such as the belief in the Resurrection, that I'm having a lot of trouble with. But none of this has anything to do with my close encounter experiences."

Strieber said the religious changes he has gone through are "typical of anyone who has a religious life at all and is concerned with the welfare of their soul."

But still he has reservations.

"I don't even know if I have a soul," he said. "I've never been sure about that. I think so, and I think so because I have a lot of evidence that suggests that something exists that is more than just the physical body. But whether that persists after the death of the body, I haven't the faintest idea."

While he professes not to know, Strieber also resists the word "agnostic."

"The word 'agnostic' is such a copout," he said. "I hate it. I'm actively searching, let's put it that way. As I say, the close encounter experience doesn't seem to be too related to religion. The Visitors never seemed to indicate any religious beliefs. They don't fit into any religious cosmology."

Strieber said that when people attempt to match the experience to religious tradition, they do so for lack of a better way to describe the aliens.

"To me," he said, "they're not demons or angels. I think the main problem that we have right now is that we can't describe them. And because we can't describe them, we keep trying to fit them into old descriptions that don't necessarily fit."

LINDA CORTILE

Linda Cortile (a pseudonym) is the focal point of the story Budd Hopkins tells in his 1996 book *Witnessed: The True Story of the Brooklyn Bridge UFO Abductions*. The New York City housewife was abducted by aliens from her high-rise apartment in full view of several witnesses, hence the book's title. Her experience was hailed as "The

Case of the Century" at the time, mainly because of all the objective proof, at least in terms of eyewitnesses, that was available to Hopkins as a researcher when he began to investigate Cortile's claims.

Like Strieber, Cortile was also raised as a Catholic.

"I've always had my faith," she said. "I was never an ultra-religious person, but I am a Roman Catholic. And I've always loved my religion."

Cortile said that God's role in her abduction experiences was to help her endure them.

"I couldn't believe I pulled through it," she said, "and am presently mentally stable. I really don't know where that strength came from. It had to come from God. And so my faith is stronger as far as religion is concerned."

Neither was it God's will that she was chosen to be an abductee.

"I don't believe God did this to me," she said. "It's just something that happened. And what had happened to me as far as aliens are concerned is as natural as life, death, and love. God gave me the strength to go through it.

"However, I don't believe religion has anything to do with the aliens," she continued. "The only religious aspect of it that I can see is that God created them, too. But I don't believe he goes around abducting people."

BUDD HOPKINS

UFO abduction researcher Budd Hopkins, the aforementioned author of *Witnessed*, has also written two other classics on alien abduction, *Missing Time* (1981) and *Intruders* (1987). Hopkins has always been a trailblazer in the field of abduction research. He was the first to uncover the alien genetic experiments that have since come to be regarded as perhaps the true purpose behind the abduction experience. He also coined the term "screen memory" to describe how the process of the amnesia imposed by the aliens works to obscure the abductees' recollection of their experience.

His answers to my questions regarding good versus evil were a little different. Hopkins replied with what I considered a rather skillful analogy.

"Is Exxon a malevolent company, or a benign, helpful, wonderful company?" he asked. "First, you start with the oil spill—there's no arguing with the oil spill. But the oil spill doesn't let you know Exxon's intentions or its moral character, its nature. One of the things I try very hard to do in both Intruders and Missing Time is to avoid a kind

Budd Hopkins

of final statement as to the nature of the UFO occupants.

"I can understand the impulse of a Whitley Strieber or a Dr. Leo Sprinkle [Sprinkle is a Wyoming UFO researcher who advocates the aliens as benevolent], or of other people who believe that there's some kind of wonderful understanding, like God loves us or something. Everybody likes to believe that even though Mommy and Daddy are wonderful and nice, somewhere out there in the sky there's somebody even nicer who really does love us and understand us. And I can understand why somebody would want this concept to be true, and as a matter of fact, I would like it to be true. Who the heck wouldn't? But that is just not what is going on. Unfortunately, there is a gap of understanding which is separate from the idea of an innate malevolence or anything of that sort."

When I asked Hopkins if there was some degree of masochism involved in these abduction experiences, he replied, "In some cases there's something of that, too. But the problem is this: if someone hurts you in some context or says something stupid to hurt your feelings, if you're normal you say to yourself something like, 'I know this person and he's ordinarily okay, and I don't know why he did this. But I don't like that aspect of him.' You don't just think all of a sudden, 'I now believe that person is a demon.' Should that same person take you out to dinner and behave very civilly toward you, you don't suddenly think, 'I thought he was just a nice, interesting person, but now I regard him as a god.' You don't translate the nature of the person just because of how you feel at the moment that he's treated you. Doing so is really to act as a child. The issue of what the UFO occupants are actually doing to us, physically and psychologically, is an issue we can address rationally and with some certainty. The innate nature of the aliens, physically, psychologically and ethically is quite another issue, and is presently unknowable."

KATHARINA WILSON

I also spoke to abductee Katharina Wilson, the author of *The Alien Jigsaw* (1995). Wilson self-published her book about her abduction experiences and managed to sell out her first printing, a testimony to the intriguing nature of the story she had to tell. Like many abductees, she comes away from the experience with a great deal of anger directed at the aliens, but she also manages to maintain an admirable level of objectivity as she struggles through whatever transformation she has been selected for.

For Wilson, church attendance began in childhood but lost its luster after she became aware she was an abductee.

"I went to church every Sunday until I was eighteen years old," Wilson said. "I don't remember ever leaving church feeling good about myself or life in general. I was made to feel guilty rather than hopeful or uplifted. I never understood that, but I knew I didn't like it."

Wilson was 21-years-old when the pivotal experience of seeing an unearthly yellow light appear in her bedroom made her doubt her sanity. She had begun attending a fundamentalist church at around the same time.

"After some bizarre conversations about whether this light was from God or Satan," she said, "and after learning about some of the people I was involved with, I realized these people were dangerous. As I look back on that time, with their attempts at trying to get me to quit college in my senior year and to disown my family and friends, I realize it was more of a cult than anything."

Wilson said that ultimately there is not much difference between the aliens and organized religion.

"Both seem to use a level of manipulation," she said, "to obtain their desired result. Churches will instill fear and guilt to obtain your money. Aliens instill fear and guilt to obtain your Will."

Like Cortile, Wilson credits God with helping her endure the trauma of abduction.

"I think living under such extreme pressures," she said, "has forced me to look to my inner strengths for survival. When my inner strength is exhausted, I am forced to reach out to that which created me: God. I am slowly gaining strength from God. I believe that God is real and that God cares."

Wilson also feels there are ways to resist an abduction experience when it is happening and to fight off the abductors using such techniques as "mental struggle," "righteous anger," and "protective rage," methods originally developed by abduction researcher Ann Druffel. In other words, to visual images and learn attitudes that drive the aliens away.

"It is important to me to add that I do not believe these techniques will work," she said, "if there is even one molecule in your body that still wants to participate—even if it's for the learning experience or for curiosity's sake. Unless every fiber in your body 'believes' you really want them out of your life, they will know it and they will come back."

Wilson also feels God offers help with the resistance process.

"Today," she said, "when I feel I may be curious about them, I concentrate on God, or the Creative Force, and I say, 'If I need answers—or if I need the truth about the phenomenon—it will come from God, not aliens.' It's a way to remind myself and the aliens that I am aware of the enormous manipulative abilities they have."

Still there is an upside to Wilson's experiences which involves the notion of "Spirituality."

"Perhaps it is that which organized religion is so severely lacking," she said. "The teaching of Spirituality, which has helped me more than anything. In some cases, my involvement with certain aliens has taken me in to the Spiritual Realm and what I believe to be other dimensions. Unlike most people on our planet, I know these realms exist. Spirituality is what is important, not religion."

PROPHECIES GIVEN TO WILSON

The abduction experience often carries with it a deep sense of responsibility. Wilson talked more about visions of the future she has received.

"Like many abductees," Wilson said, "I feel a great weight upon me, as if I am preparing for an important event to take place. I also feel as if I am, in part, responsible for something very important. I want to make it very clear that I do not feel special because of my experiences. Quite the contrary. I feel an enormous burden because of these experiences, and rather than feeling I've been 'chosen,' I feel as if it is my duty or my assignment to help educate people about this phenomenon."

That burdensome sense of responsibility also includes receiving frightening visions of the Earth's future and mankind's own powerlessness in the face of global nuclear and environmental disaster.

"In early 1995," Wilson said, "I had a vision of nuclear war that I documented in an unpublished paper called '*Curious Correlations*.' The vision showed that China will attack both Russia and the United States with nuclear weapons. They will be carried by red, high performance jets belonging to the Chinese military. Nuclear weapons and oil are going to be the main 'tools' of this war.

"How do I feel about visions such as these?" Wilson continued. "First, I have no idea why I'm receiving information such as this, unless I'm supposed to share it with others. It does me no personal good to have to live with this knowledge, if that is indeed what

37

it is. Second, I don't want anything like this to occur, and my life isn't so boring that I would create something like this to make it more interesting. As to the 'reality' of these visions, I can only describe them as being absolutely 'powerful.' When you see these events unfolding before you, at that moment, you have no choice but to believe them."

I asked her if she had received any other visions about the future of mankind.

"I was given a vision of 'humanity,'" she replied. "'Humanity' was standing in line inside a mall at a burger joint, content with their minimum wage jobs. They weren't striving for anything more in life. They weren't trying to educate themselves. They weren't trying to make a positive difference. They were satisfied. A short, pudgy female Being with dark skin and funny looking glasses was standing next to me. She was telepathically tuning into my thoughts and feelings. I said to her, 'I can't believe they're satisfied with this. Eating animals and existing to work . . . . it's unacceptable.' The female telepathically replied, matter-of-factly, 'They are receptacles.'"

"With these three words," Wilson continued, "her thoughts poured into my mind. In an instant she told me that what I was calling 'unacceptable' was all that these people's souls were capable of experiencing. I also felt her say something about their future; that their future and my future would be very different. I wasn't a part of them. I wasn't connected to 'humanity.'"

This has been a discussion of the good versus evil elements of abduction as perceived by many of the more widely known abductees and researchers. Obviously, there has been a wide range of opinions expressed here, and certainly the field is open to as many different beliefs as there are people having the experience.

Chapter Four
Dr. R. Leo Sprinkle And Benevolent Aliens

"My own feeling is that we're already a part of heaven. We think of Earth and heaven as separate, but we're part of it. My hope is that before my lifetime runs out for me, that we will hear that uttered by whoever's in charge, whether it's by the United Nations or whoever the representatives are, that they announce that heaven and Earth have joined. That will be exciting. I'll jump up and click my heels if I'm able."

Dr. R. Leo Sprinkle has been on the vanguard of UFO research for more than forty years. His reputation as a compassionate investigator has few equals in the field, and his heartfelt belief that both the aliens and mankind are basically benevolent provides some much needed encouragement for everyone who has been touched by the UFO mystery.

Sprinkle was born and raised in Rocky Ford, Colorado. He attended the University of Colorado at Boulder, where he earned his Masters Degree, then received his Ph.D. in counseling psychology at the University of Missouri in 1961. His wife Marilyn and he have four grown children.

"I feel like if I haven't done anything else," Sprinkle said, "I've helped raise four grand people."

Sprinkle taught at the University of North Dakota in Grand Forks from 1961 to 1964. He moved on to the University of Wyoming in Laramie, where he taught until 1989.

"I left the university to go into part-time private practice," he said, "in order to preserve my health and sanity. I couldn't handle the pressure at the university regarding my studies in reincarnation and UFO investigations."

Which is an obvious sign of Sprinkle's dedication both to the esoteric disciplines of UFO and reincarnation research as well as to the experiencers he has helped along the way.

LEO SPRINKLE'S FIRST UFO EXPERIENCES

How did Sprinkle first discover UFOs? Or maybe one should ask, how did UFOs first find him?

"My first conscious recollection," he said, "was a sighting of a flying saucer in 1949. A buddy, Joe Wagner, and I saw a flying saucer over the Arts and Sciences building

Dr. R. Leo Sprinkle

at the University of Colorado in Boulder. I changed from a scoffer to a skeptic. Then my wife and I had a sighting over Boulder as we were driving back from Denver in 1956, and I changed from a skeptic to a believer. I knew then that I had work to do, to investigate.

"Then finally," he continued, "when I was fifty years old, I had the courage to do what other people had previously done. I had worked since 1967 with hypnotic techniques, to help people recall more about their encounters. So in 1980, I went back in memory to what seemed to be a childhood experience. I was ten years old, in 1940, and feeling that I was onboard a craft with a tall man on my left with his arm around my shoulder and telling me, 'Leo, learn to read and write well. When you grow up, you can help other people learn more about their purpose in life.'"

Sprinkle said his reaction at the time was typical of many psychologists. He reserved a certain amount of skepticism about the childhood memory and felt it could still be a fantasy or a daydream. But ten years later, the memory would return with great emotional force.

"In 1990," he explained, "in front of 150 people at our UFO conference, I sobbed as I recognized that the recollection was not only true, but it was part of my inner self. I was listening to a woman named Marika Shields, out of Denver, and she was talking about her UFO experiences and an encounter with a little E.T. with leggings and footwear just like a kid's pajamas, all in one. And I started to sob as I was recalling that the guy's uniform that I remembered as a ten-year-old onboard a craft was that same way, the leggings and the shoe just fit together. So I told myself, okay, I no longer have the luxury of being skeptical. I know that it happened.

"So I accept it as an indication that not only am I a contactee, but that probably the guy's message is correct," he went on. "Of course by that time I had learned to do what I consider 'psychological resonance,' or what other people call 'life readings,' where I provide information to people that seems to be meaningful to them in terms of their purpose in life. So whether these things happened or not, nevertheless it's been a marvelous journey."

In 1999, Sprinkle published a book called *Soul Samples*, which he said provides a sketch of his own experiences as well as summarizes the data he had collected over the years from people in reincarnation and UFO workshops and from individuals who had been willing to undergo hypnosis with him to relive and remember their own encounters.

TWO APPROACHES TO THE ALIENS' BENEVOLENCE

How can we know whether the aliens are truly benevolent and have our best interests at heart when they abduct or otherwise interact with us? Sprinkle said there are two arguments that can lead an experiencer to that conclusion.

"One argument is," he began, "that if the universe is alive with intelligent life, then by whatever the time periods are, there would be so many civilizations that would have to depend on cooperative ventures that whatever wars there would have been over territory or whatever would be completed by now. So if there are enough resources throughout the universe for people to house and shelter themselves and to travel and look around, then they would inevitably develop a cooperative society even if there are cases of violence here and there. Therefore a philosophical argument could be made that the many civilizations would have to learn to cooperate with one another, otherwise they'd die out through subjugating one another and killing one another."

In other words, given that the many alien civilizations haven't died out through warfare with one another on their way here, they must have learned benevolent ways purely as a means of simple survival.

The other approach deals with the stories told by abductees and experiencers themselves.

"The second basic argument comes from people," Sprinkle said, "who claim to have E.T. encounters. Although there are some cases of people being injured and dying as a result of encounters, most of the people that I've worked with and talked with and the reports I've read from all over the planet, indicate that the interactions—if not benevolent—are at least peaceful. Or at the very least, 'objective, scientific, technical,' those kinds of interactions where people say that somebody is doing a job and that they aren't severely harming the humans that they're dealing with.

"So I think those two arguments," he continued, "the philosophical argument and the encounter-based experiences are indications that there's little hostility that is exhibited by the entities. In fact, many times they seem to put themselves at risk in getting away from people who are firing at them or whatever. There are people who claim healings at the hands of E.T.s. That would be the strongest argument for a benevolent attitude on the part of E.T.s.   There are many reports of people who claim that they have not only been helped physically, medically, but I also work with people who claim that their encounters with E.T.s have helped them get a deeper perspective on life and on themselves. They have had psychic gifts presented to them, or developed within them. So all of those arguments to me provide a basis for believing the E.T.s are benevolent."

SELF-EXAMINATION AND REINCARNATION

Sprinkle recounted the tale of a woman he worked with who was led to a most revealing self-discovery through a contact experience.

"A Denver psychotherapist felt like she went back to a lifetime as an Egyptian priestess," Sprinkle said. "In that lifetime, she was bitten by an insect and poisoned. Well, in this lifetime she wakes up in the morning and her eye is puffy. She goes to the mirror, she pulls out a little something, and later tries to give it to some investigators to see if it would show anything extraterrestrial."

The woman reported "dreaming" or experiencing E.T.s hovering around her and putting the object in her eye in order for her to relive that lifetime as a priestess and to "recall" that she was seeing things correctly. Sprinkle pointed out that the object was inserted in her right eye, an intended play on words that she was seeing things "right."

"She was told that she didn't need to fear death from the puffy eye," Sprinkle said, "but what it did was remind her that she serves as a priestess in this lifetime, helping others.

"So many of the stories that people describe to me about being examined on a table, it's as if it's not only a physical experience in their memory, but it's also symbolic. It's as if they are examining themselves with the help of E.T.s and saying, 'What kind of life am I living? Am I on the right path?' So it's a spiritual initiation into a new way of looking at themselves and moving into a new culture—that they are part of an intergalactic or a cosmic culture, not just a human being on the planet Earth."

SPRINKLE MEETS ARTHUR C. CLARKE

Sprinkle also told the story of his meeting with Arthur C. Clarke, the author of numerous works of science-fiction, including the blockbuster *2001: A Space Odyssey*. Clarke had come to the University of Wyoming on a lecture tour, and the students, knowing of Sprinkle's interest in UFOs, had asked him to introduce Clarke. Clarke and Sprinkle were standing together offstage when Sprinkle broached the obvious question to Clarke.

"I said, 'Pardon me sir, but what's your take on the UFO/flying saucer scenario?' And he said, 'Well, it's important or unimportant, depending on your attitude.' He was very arrogant. And I said, 'Do you mind telling me what you mean by that?'"

Clarke employed the analogy of a highway sign. The sign is a stick of wood or a piece of metal with a symbol on it.

"Now the stick of wood or the piece of metal," Sprinkle explained, "that's not very important. But the symbol could be important, if it's 'Bridge Out' or 'Danger Ahead' or 'Detour' or whatever. So he said flying saucers are important or unimportant depending upon what they symbolize. But they do symbolize something. They're the signs of the time. He also said that he and Stanley Kubrick, the night they were planning the movie *2001*, had a UFO sighting. I thought, 'Wow, that's good timing.'"

SPRINKLE DISCUSSES PROPHECY

When I asked Sprinkle for his views on E.T.s and prophecy, he again came at the question with a two-pronged approach.

"There have been a whole bunch of little prophecies," he said, "which usually don't turn out. Like someone says, 'Oh, the aliens told me to bring the reporters to the hill where I saw them last week and they'll reappear.' Then the people come up there and they *don't* reappear.

"So prophecy to me represents two different kinds of issues. Some people think of prophecy as a prediction, and so a lot of the predictions don't hold true. But if one takes the point of view that prophecy is a warning, you know, like the mother who says to the little kid, 'Watch out, if you don't stop riding your bicycle without using your hands, you're going to fall off. You're going to hit your head, your eyeball will pop out and roll down the street and into the river and into the ocean and the fish will eat it.' Well, it's not that the mother is *predicting* that that's going to happen, but she is warning the child that it *might* happen if he doesn't sit up and ride his bicycle the way he should. In the same way, the prophecies to me are not so much predictions as they are warnings and guidance."

The aliens' ultimate intent for the future of Earth is also a two-pronged program, according to Sprinkle.

"One is to help humanity rejuvenate the planet," he said, "and the other is to help humanity in its next stage of evolution. And those two general statements make sense to me. I interpret it as meaning to restore the balance of masculine and feminine science. Feminine science is nurturing, and masculine science is exploring. We've used masculine science now for some few hundred years, and it's been corrupted to the point of not only exploring but exploiting. Now if we balance the sciences with nurturing as well as exploring, then I think we'll be able to possibly regain the health of the planet.

"The other interpretation, to help humanity in its next stage of evolution, I believe that refers to a psychic or spiritual evolution. My bias is that the planet is the physical world, our bodies are the biological world, our minds are the psychological world, and our souls are the spiritual world. We have learned a lot about the nature of the body and the mind, and now it's time to learn about the soul."

Most of the predictions made in recent years really come from a quite human source, not from the aliens themselves, Sprinkle said.

"I don't know anybody who said that they had been told by E.T.s that there would be another world war or the Antichrist would come and those kinds of things. But a lot of humans have said that."

WHERE THE "NEGATIVE" ALIENS FIT IN

In the picture of benevolent aliens kindly guiding our evolution that Sprinkle so optimistically paints, where do the so-called "negative" aliens fit?

"I think of the reptilians and the insectoids and the others as human drama characters," he explained. "Nancy Kooney [a correspondent of Sprinkle's] in her letter to me years ago said it very nicely. She said that her reading of the literature would suggest that the different entities play different roles, whether it's something warlike or something dealing with sexuality or whatever. Different entities come to us for different games or different dramas. So it's like going from one classroom to another. Just like going from one college to another and then you finally get a picture of the university."

Sprinkle also made another comparison, drawn from his many years of research, positing that the true E.T.s are higher forces, humans are the sheep and the small gray aliens are the sheepdogs.

"If we follow the shepherds," he said, "then all is well. Otherwise, the sheepdogs come after the sheep and nip at our heels and it hurts. So it's the cliché that some people don't learn by seeing the light, they learn by feeling the heat. To me, the so-called negative aliens or the negative E.T. experiences are designed to be a wakeup call.

They're like the probation officer or the hooky officer who comes to the kids who aren't learning, who aren't shaping up. To my way of thinking, it's an educational process."

But Sprinkle allowed for the possibility that he may be wrong.

"It may well be that there *are* bad E.T.s," he said, "who are dedicated to service to self, and who are fighting the good E.T.s who are dedicated to service to others. And humans are caught in the middle."

"Which is all eventually resolved, Sprinkle feels, by the process of reincarnation.

If there is conflict, if there is violence, if there is destruction, then the soul comes back and learns how to play the more benevolent game because in the long-run that's more fun."

ARE WE ALREADY THERE?

When I asked Sprinkle where he felt our relationship with the aliens will lead us in the future, he surprised me by saying he felt we were already there.

"My view is that we already are part of a cosmic culture," he said, "even if we're not aware of it. The metaphor that comes to my mind is that we're like a little neighborhood of armed kids who don't want the social workers and the policemen to come in, so we threaten each other to keep quiet and don't talk about the E.T.s because we don't think of ourselves as 'they,' we think of ourselves as 'us.' So it's us against them.

"But my own feeling is that we're already a part of heaven. We think of Earth and heaven as separate, but we're part of it. My hope is that before my lifetime runs out for me, that we will hear that uttered by whoever's in charge, whether it's by the United Nations or whoever the representatives are, that they announce that heaven and Earth have joined. That will be exciting. I'll jump up and click my heels if I'm able."

In the meantime, Sprinkle had some advice for people who feel they have encountered aliens and are having ongoing experiences with them.

"I encourage people who've had E.T. encounters to keep a journal and decide whether to share it with others. I encourage them to meditate each day and then to meditate on the question, 'What can I learn from you guys? What's the lesson involved in this encounter?' Then they get a different set of instructors. Instead of tormenters, they get mentors. I encourage people to tell themselves that if they are learning and growing, then they're moving up in levels of consciousness.

"So it seems to me," Sprinkle concluded, "that regardless of whether the E.T.s are good, bad or indifferent, if we learn from our experiences, then we benefit. I'd like to encourage people to benefit from their experiences themselves, regardless of whether they're able to share it with others. The hope is that eventually they will be able to share it with others, and then as others share their experiences, then all together as humanity we will rise in consciousness. That's my hope."

First Night photo

picture was taken From Kfar Saba, UFO over Kohav Yair.

Chapter Five
Heaven's Gate: How Some True Believers Got It Wrong

"It's my understanding that there is actually another level of existence beyond this one. We call it the 'Next Level.' Some people call it heaven. And it may actually have a different name than that once you get there. We are not privy to that information. But 'Next Level' is fine.

"Paradise is different for everyone," he continued, "but my understanding is that it's a physical place. It's not like an ethereal place. It's not like everything's made of vapor. You know? It's real, tangible stuff. It's different than human, different than our physics might be, but still in its own way it's physical."

At the outset, it is conceded that the Heaven's Gate suicides took place more than five years ago and that those events are not exactly a front-page story anymore. But this book seeks to make its case for the true aliens as benevolent, caring entities who would never lead their Chosen Ones to the kind of tragic self-sacrifice that the 39 cult members "chose" for themselves.

It is an equally obvious point that the extreme religious fanaticism that drove Heaven's Gate to make its dramatic escape from the Earthly plane by suicide is similar in form and intensity to the fanaticism that fuels the fires of Osama bin Laden and his many terrorist henchmen. Both Heaven's Gate and the terrorists saw suicide as a true form of martyrdom, a simple method of instantly entering the Gates of Paradise by means of self-inflicted death.

The entire UFO community still bears the stain of the Heaven's Gate suicides. Serious researchers and genuine abductees continue to find themselves tarred with the same brush, even though they had no links to the tragedy. It is therefore necessary to revisit the Heaven's Gate suicides and attempt to understand the events of that spring day in 1997 in the context of the things that this book is concerned with, UFOs, prophecy and the End of Time.

A REVIEW OF THE EVENTS SURROUNDING THE SUICIDES

In a mansion in the exclusive Rancho Santa Fe section of San Diego, the suicides took place in three separate waves, beginning on the Saturday or Sunday before Easter, on or around March 23, 1997. The first group of fifteen members swallowed applesauce or pudding laced with Phenobarbital and washed it down with vodka. Some of them covered their heads with plastic bags that were secured with elastic bands. Other members then cleaned up and covered the dead with purple shrouds.

The following day, Monday the 24th, fifteen more died and were covered with shrouds. On Tuesday, the remaining cultists killed themselves and the last two disposed of the others' plastic bags.

That same Tuesday morning, Rio DiAngelo, a cult member who had defected some months earlier, received a FedEx package at work that contained a letter and two videotapes. Though the package was meant to arrive on Wednesday, it arrived a day early. Still, DiAngelo did not open it until Tuesday night.

On Wednesday, March 26, DiAngelo still had not watched the tapes. Nevertheless, he told his boss, Nick Matzorkis, that he thought the group was dead. Around 10 AM, Matzorkis drove DiAngelo to the house. He came out 20 minutes later, having seen the bodies. At 1:30 PM that afternoon, Matzorkis and DiAngelo called the police anonymously to tell them to check the house.

At 3:30 PM, Deputy Robert Brunk of the San Diego County Sheriff's Department arrived. He opened a side door, smelled a pungent odor and called for backup. When Deputy Laura Gaceck arrived, the two officers put on surgical masks and went in. After they counted 10 bodies, they radioed their findings to the homicide unit.

THE EARLY DAYS OF "THE TWO"

Marshall Herf Applewhite met his partner and co-leader Bonnie Lu Trusdale Nettles in 1970. She was working as a nurse in the mental hospital Applewhite checked himself into after leaving his job as a music teacher at a small Roman Catholic school in Houston, Texas. College records from the time state that he left due to "health problems of an emotional nature."

Nettles dabbled in astrology, mysticism and far-out religious movements. Meanwhile, Applewhite claimed to have recently had a "near-death-experience" after a heart attack. They quickly became very close friends, and the relationship remained platonic throughout their years together as part of their determination to completely rid themselves of earthly "base desires."

The pair gave each other nicknames that changed over time. At one point, they called themselves "Bo" and "Peep," which was a play on words that made reference to "Little Bo Peep," the shepherd of their flock. Their final names for one another were "Do" and

"Ti," notes on the musical scale in a celestial symphony.

But they also called themselves "The Two," after the two witnesses in the Book of Revelation who prophesy for a period of time before being slain by the Antichrist and then are resurrected and ascend to Heaven before a world that watches in amazement. The agent of that ascension was to be a cloud of light—a UFO. The Two began to gain followers after holding a series of public meetings in which they preached their Christian ideology mixed with references to aliens and spaceships, first receiving national attention after a meeting in Waldport, Oregon, in 1975.

THE CULT AND ITS PRACTICES

When the UFO that The Two prophesied failed to materialize, the group lost numerous members, many of whom left accusing The Two of mind control games. Negative publicity soon followed, and the group went into the wilderness to recoup its losses.

Those followers who did stay began to live according to a strict regimen that required abstinence from alcohol, drugs and sex. Members were required to check in with their leader every 12 minutes. Everyone was given a "check partner" to guard against backsliding and independent thought. Doubters were sent to a "decontamination zone."

"Ti" died in 1985 of liver cancer. "Do" declared that she had become a "more advanced member of the Next Level" and that he hoped to eventually join her. Then in 1993, his cult reemerged under the name Heaven's Gate when Applewhite took out a newspaper ad in *USA Today* that was headlined "UFO Cult Resurfaces With Final Offer." According to the advertisement, this was "the last chance to advance beyond human."

In the ad, the cult acknowledged its philosophical ties to other millennial groups such as the Branch Davidians and the Solar Temple, as well as the enemy the groups had in common: the corrupt world believed to be ruled by the Devil.

THE CULT'S FINAL PHASE

In 1996, the Heaven's Gate cult started a business called Higher Source Contract Enterprises, a web page design company. By offering cheap rates and up-to-date design, the company lured clients like the San Diego Polo Club and a specialty car parts store called The British Masters.

The cult earned enough from its business to live in the $7000-a-month mansion in the upscale Rancho Santa Fe section of San Diego where their bodies were found. They followed a daily routine of rising before 4 AM to gaze into the night sky at their true home in the heavens, then had a simple group meal, typically of pasta. For the rest of the day, the group would subsist on fruit, lemonade and Diet Coke while they worked designing web pages.

At the same time, "Do" began to use the Internet to recruit new members by sending messages with titles like "Time To Die For God?" to news groups that focus on suicide, depression and substance abuse. The cult's membership doubled, according to "Do," who assured his followers they were heaven-sent souls who had been chosen to fight against "the Luciferian" enemies of God.

In spite of the gains in membership, the group was unable to sell a movie treatment about its story to Hollywood. There was increasing paranoia among members about an attack from the government as well. And the general public's indifference to the cult was construed as a "signal to begin our preparations to return home."

When the group learned that a UFO "four times the size of Earth" was reportedly following in the wake of the Hale-Bopp comet, it was thought that their beloved "Ti" was returning to Earth to take them home with her. The comet drew ever closer, and as Holy Week approached, the cultists prepared to shed their "earthly container," celebrating with a final meal of chicken potpie and cheesecake.

THE IMAGES THAT REMAINED

In the videotapes left behind, some of the cult members actually seemed giddy. One woman chirped, "We're looking forward to this," while another sang, "Beam me up!"

According to University of North Carolina religious teacher Jim Tabor, who was involved in the last desperate attempts to communicate with David Koresh by radio, "This group is completely different. These people rather calmly followed suicide as their exit, in a very positive way, to a higher level of existence. They define death not as the enemy of life but as life itself."

Also on that farewell video is one woman who says, "We couldn't be happier about what we're going to do." A man in his forties says, "I've been looking forward to this for so long." A woman, laughing slightly, says, "People in the world who thought I'd completely lost my marbles—they're not right. I couldn't have made a better choice."

However, other cult experts warned at the time that the public should not be taken in by the cheerful departures nor by the notion that it was a small group of people exercising their free will.

"I don't consider it suicide. I consider it murder," said Janja Lalich, a cult expert who had been monitoring Heaven's Gate since 1994 after several distraught parents contacted her with worries about their missing children.

"[Applewhite] controlled it; he called the shots," Lalich said. "These people were pawns in his personal fantasy."

[This introductory review section was based in part on reports from the April 17, 1997, issues of **TIME** and **Newsweek** magazines.]

A SURVIVOR SPEAKS

About a year after the Heaven's Gate suicides occurred, I received a press release from a publicist I had worked with for a few years. She was promoting a new book called *How and When Heaven's Gate May Be Entered* (1997 by the Telah Foundation), and offered to set up an interview with Rio DiAngelo, the survivor of the cult who led police to the bodies.

As it turned out, I was one of the few journalists to take the publicist up on her offer. CNN talk show host Larry King, for instance, at first agreed to have DiAngelo appear on his program, but later declined because he felt the book being promoted wasn't timely enough.

In any case, I did interview DiAngelo by phone that spring of 1998, and I got some very interesting answers to many nagging questions. According to the press release, DiAngelo hoped to tell the "other side of the story" to a non-comprehending world.

So my first question to him was, "What is that other side of the story?"

"Basically, it seems that most people," DiAngelo said, "know about the people who exited their vehicles. The media calls it suicide. We looked at it differently, but that's really what the media has focused on. And they've focused on people's fear of death. So what I'm here to help people understand is that there's more to it than that. The bottom line is that these people had discovered some things, some information that Do brought to this planet that perhaps had not been available for about 2,000 years. It contained stuff that Jesus was talking about, I have come to discover."

Did DiAngelo feel the cult had really gone on to a heavenly place? He answered with an unequivocal Yes, but also tried to clarify exactly what that meant.

"Now a heavenly place," he began, "not ethereal, not imaginary, not fantasy, but a real place. It's my understanding that there is actually another level of existence beyond this one. We call it the 'Next Level.' Some people call it heaven. And it may actually have a different name than that once you get there. We are not privy to that information. But 'Next Level' is fine.

"Paradise is different for everyone," he continued, "but my understanding is that it's a physical place. It's not like an ethereal place. It's not like everything's made of vapor. You know? It's real, tangible stuff. It's different than human, different than our physics might be, but still in its own way it's physical."

But he still shied away from the act of suicide himself. Why?

"Because reincarnation is a factor," he replied. "So what happens when you end your life here, you pick up in the next life where you left off. It makes sense to me that a person would want to get as far as possible in this particular lifetime."

Meanwhile, DiAngelo's fellow members in "The Class" had already reached the point where they needed to evolve no more.

"We developed our soul," he said, "so that we had actually become different than the body and different than the spirit. We actually became the soul. And the soul is what takes you from here to there. As far as a moral thing, these people were done with all their lessons. They don't need to come back to this Earth anymore. They're done. There's no reason to stay here."

Therefore, the right way to proceed, according to DiAngelo, is to "Stick around and learn new lessons as long as possible until you get to the point where you meet up with a representative from the 'Next Level' and then follow those instructions and go to the 'Next Level.'"

One of the questions that played on my mind throughout the interview was whether DiAngelo or the other members of the cult had ever actually had any of the more common UFO experiences. Had they ever had a typical abduction experience, or even sighted a ship?

"None of them, to my knowledge, had had an abduction experience," he said. "However, I clearly remember one time when we were living in this place in Tucson, and during the night there were some classmates who actually saw what we call

'Next-Level-Beings' in the room with us, checking on different ones in the class. They explained their experiences as very interesting, very unusual."

DiAngelo also talked about his departure from the cult, a decision which would eventually save his life.

"It was quite interesting," he said, "because I was ready to go with them. And then I had what I call a type of 'intuition,' which is something that's telling you something that you need to pay attention to, something that might not be in your consciousness. I feel that an intuition led me to the class in the first place, and made me realize this 'information' was familiar. That same intuition was telling me that there was something to do geographically away from the class, something that needed to be done. I was given the option to accept, or I could go with them. It was my choice.

"So I talked to Do about it," he continued, "and it was extremely emotional. I was very confused. I didn't want to go. I didn't want to leave the class at all. I wanted to be with them. But he told me it looked like it was part of a plan and that, if I was willing to accept it, then he would condone it. So I did."

WAS THE CULT'S DOCTRINE SOUND?

When reading and listening to reports of the theological and philosophical beliefs of the Heaven's Gate cult, many people were struck by how the group's ideas resembled those of early Christians and echoed with common practices from throughout history. What may seem on the surface to be the lunacy of a modern day cult and its leader has a strong connection with earlier spiritual traditions.

Perhaps the most widely read and innovative scholar of the early Christian Church is Elaine Pagels, Ph.D., who has written several books on Gnostic Christianity (*The Gnostic Gospels*, 1979), the role of women in the Bible (*Adam, Eve and the Serpent*, 1988), and the changing perceptions of the Devil over the centuries spanned by scripture (*The Origin of Satan*, 1995). I spoke to Dr. Pagels about a month after the Heaven's Gate suicides had occurred and she offered up a wealth of information that confirmed a philosophical and religious link between the cult and numerous practices and beliefs of Christianity in its infancy.

"I think it's true," she said, "that most of what I've read about this movement is really not very different from the early Christian movement in most of its respects. Many of the teachings about renouncing family and sexuality and so forth are quite consistent with Christian teaching. You can see that the leader of this movement had a father who was a preacher. He seems to know the New Testament quite well.

"What I find quite different," Pagels went on, "is that most Christian groups would never invest in a human being today the kind of supernatural qualities that this group seems to have invested in their leader or leaders. And second, suicide has never been a positive option in Christian tradition so far as I know it. Martyrdom was a pretty extreme situation. If you said you were a Christian, you could get killed. Some people thought you were killing yourself if you admitted it, but that's an extreme view.

"The word 'martyr' means 'witness. And they were witnessing to what they believed. I think that's quite different from believing that suicide offers access to the 'Next Level.' *That* I've never seen in any Christian teaching."

I also asked about the group's hatred of the human body as the unclean prison of the soul. I said I had thought it was basically a Gnostic doctrine, but Pagels corrected me on that point.

"That's what many people say about Gnostic teaching," she said, "and there are some ancient texts that support that. However, you can get a similar view from parts of the New Testament where Paul speaks about his longing to be absent from the body and present with the Lord. He speaks about subduing the flesh and so forth. There are similar sort of antagonistic views of the body in perfectly straight-forward Christian tradition. In fact, in most ancient traditions. And you find it in philosophic sources as well. It's a very commonplace view."

I next asked about a section of the New Testament, Matthew Chapter 19, which dealt with the subject of eunuchs, with Jesus saying that sometimes men where eunuchs for "the sake of the Kingdom of Heaven." The men of the Heaven's Gate cult apparently took that bit of scripture quite literally. They did not simply abstain, but made it physically impossible for them to do otherwise.

"Everyone in the ancient church," Pagels said, "who commented on that thought—and had no question—but that he was praising those who made themselves eunuchs for the sake of the Kingdom of God. It was just assumed that this was a good thing to do. It was considered also to be very hard, but Fathers of the early Church admired people who castrated themselves."

So how do you feel, I asked her, that the castrations of Marshall Applewhite and several of his followers fit with what Christ said? Were they taking an obscure saying too much to heart?

"It depends how literally you want to take those sayings," she said. "I know of cases in which a convert to Christianity took literally the saying from the Gospel, 'If your eye offends you, pluck it out.' I've known of someone who tore his eye out because he thought he was obeying the command of Christ. That kind of literal response to what most of us consider a sort of hyperbolic and metaphoric way of speaking is certainly not one I would endorse. It's a way of speaking about removing obstructions."

Many of the cult's practices are widely shared with other institutions, rules that separate the believer from the world outside, including the breaking of family ties, the taking of a new name, the abstinence from sex, drugs and alcohol, rules of enforced silence and obedience in even the tiniest details of everyday life. Pagels agreed with me.

"Everything you mentioned," she said, "is sort of a standard way of life for many monastics around the world. Christian monastics, whether they're Roman Catholic or Orthodox or whatever. There's a book that might be useful here. It's Irving Goffman's book. He's a sociologist, and the book is called **Total Institutions**. He was a psychiatrist writing about mental hospitals. But his book talks about the methods that Total Institutions use to break down a previous sense of self and transform the self. The examples that he has in mind primarily are the Army, the monastery, prisons and mental hospitals. All of these use the same techniques. I mean there's certain ways you do that. You deprive people of the objects and possessions that are personal and so forth."

I asked, as I always do in an interview, whether there was anything Dr. Pagels wished to add.

"Well, I think this episode is very sad," she said. "I feel sorrow about this event. It seems to me that other people who feel that way might consider that the sort of denial of spiritual and religious impulses, which is common among people who regard themselves as agnostics or 'rational, sensible, scientifically minded' people, can open people up to religious points of view that are quite extreme. How shall we say? I just think that many people express surprise at this sort of event, which I think is quite sad. But in fact, it seems to me that when people are unaware that there is such a thing as spiritual need among human beings, they become perhaps more susceptible to anyone who claims to fulfill those kinds of needs. [The suppression of religious impulses] may allow for people to be much more susceptible to this kind of movement.

"I wonder how many of those people chose between that and say, the local Pentecostal Church or Roman Catholic Charismatics or a Benedictine Monastery or

Buddhist Ashram? There are many ways to explore and fulfill religious needs, I think. But many people are unaware that they have them. I think that is also unfortunate. I also think there are some people who don't either have or feel those needs in the way I'm describing. But some do, and we ought to keep that in mind."

So it fulfills a need? I asked.

"I think so," she concluded. "If you believe Freud, it just fulfills a totally neurotic need. But I don't agree with Freud. I think that religious impulses are deeper than that and more pervasive. Finding some relationship with one's self and the universe. This obviously fulfilled that for some of these people. I don't mean it fulfilled it in a way that you and I would find positive necessarily. I think it's unfortunate, but what they did is not so different, as you've rightly discerned, from many other religious traditions. I think that when people are unaware that they have religious needs they become susceptible to leaders who claim to fulfill them and who may in fact not."

A HINT OF THE SUPERNATURAL

Another interview I conducted that spring of 1997 was with UFO researcher and author Hayden Hewes. Hewes first made the acquaintance of Do and Ti in 1974, when the Mysterious Two were living in a cabin outside of Oklahoma City, Oklahoma.

At the time, Hewes was writing a column about UFOs for one of the tabloids, and the cult leaders sought him out hoping to obtain publicity for their movement in order to gain new members. At the time, the duo went by the names "Herf" and "Bonnie."

"Their message was," Hewes said, "that they were here to show how to overcome death and ascend to the 'Next Level.' [Herf also] said, 'I am alien to the Earth and will graduate to a higher plane.'"

Hewes said he was intrigued by the claims that Herf made.

"What makes him different," Hewes asked himself, "from the last person who told me they were an alien to the Earth? I found him very warm, charming, but showing little emotion. Mesmerizing in the sense that he kept his voice about the same level while talking. He usually talked in the third person, and he was very knowledgeable about religion."

Hewes would ultimately write a book about the cult, along with veteran paranormal writer Brad Steiger, called ***UFO Missionaries Extraordinary***, first published in 1976 and later reissued as ***Inside Heaven's Gate*** in the wake of the suicides.

What did Hewes himself think of Herf's claim of being an alien?

"One of the things that made me wonder," Hewes said, "if perhaps Herf might be telling the truth is that when he left my office, I shook his hand, said goodbye, then turned around and walked three or four feet. I turned back around and the man was gone. He had no way to go either way. I could not understand, and still don't, how he disappeared the way he did.

In playing our interviews back, he said quite clearly that they have the power to change their vibratory rate, which can make them disappear at will. Now, that didn't prove to me that he was an alien, but it made it a little extraordinary.

"He also told me that if I ever wanted to contact him," Hewes continued, "to 'pray towards' him with a secret code. I did not do that until 14 months later when, after hearing of the Waldport Meeting [the 1975 incident that garnered the group national publicity], I directed a message to him. The next morning, I received a call from one of his followers saying, 'You have asked, and now they have asked me to get a hold of you and let you know they will get back to answer your questions.' Now I just fell over. It was a telepathic communication across the United States where they responded the next day. And again, that's not proof, but by the same token it made me sit and wonder."

Still another strange incident occurred that Hewes could not explain.

"He was so familiar to me," Hewes said. "I couldn't put my finger on it. Why did I know this man, and where did I know him from? Well, it wasn't for some time that I happened to have a picture of him on my desk. At the same time, I had a copy of a book [Brad Steiger and I] published back in 1970 entitled *The Aliens*. It was illustrated by Hal Crawford and it dealt with the three most commonly reported occupants. The following year, **The National Enquirer** ran part of the text in an interview, along with an illustration of the second most commonly reported occupant. Well, when you put those two together, the picture of Herf Applewhite and the illustration of the UFO alien four years previous, it's an exact overlay. So here I've got a man standing in front of me saying, 'I'm an alien to the Earth,' and it matches what our research showed four years prior.

"Is that three coincidences? Is that synchronicity?" Hewes wondered aloud. "I don't know. One of the things that kept the story open as far as we were concerned was, 'Hey, maybe there's something to what they're saying.' But I know Brad and I didn't envision it would take 20-some years to get an end to the story that started in 1974."

Rio DiAngelo also had a story to tell about the possible supernatural abilities of Marshall Herf Applewhite.

"I hadn't witnessed him disappearing," DiAngelo recalled. "But I know that there were some in the class who had said something about that. They said that all of a sudden he appeared out of nowhere and there he was with his helpers and everything. Then when he left, he just disappeared. They could see him, but people who were not in the class couldn't see him for some reason. I don't know why. So I had heard people talk about that but I had never experienced it. Perhaps they were on the same wavelength, or the same vibration that he was on and was teaching them about. They were maybe just a step above the 'human eye,' so to speak, or human perception."

Did "Do" possess some kind of mystical, supernatural powers to go along with his gifts as a preacher and a leader? Is that how he inspired such a fanatic loyalty in his followers that they were willing to accompany him even in the act of suicide?

BUDD HOPKINS AND THE PRAGMATIC APPROACH

I also interviewed UFO abduction researcher Budd Hopkins that same year in order to get his opinions on the Heaven's Gate suicides. I've known Budd for more than ten years, and I already knew about his impatience regarding any sort of religious interpretation of UFOs and their alien occupants. So his answers to my questions didn't surprise me.

"The issue here is of course," Hopkins said, "that for any religious cult or group to assume that the unknown 'next life,' whatever that may be, or if it may be, is going to be superior to what we have now—that's always an exasperating idea to me."

Hopkins related a story about his appearance, soon after the tragedy, on a television program along with a group of abductees, writers and researchers.

"On the telephone line for this television station," Hopkins began, "was a man who said he was a member of the cult and that he was going to commit suicide. He didn't put it that way. He said 'leave his container' or whatever the term was. Of course everyone was pleading with him not to do it. He had a thirteen-year-old son he mentioned, and the son wasn't quite reconciled to his father leaving everybody. We were doing what we could to try to talk this man out of it.

"But the interesting point was," Hopkins continued, "one of the people on the program said, 'Have you ever talked to the UFO occupants? Spoken to them yourself?'

And he said, 'No.' He was asked, 'Have you ever been inside a UFO?' And he said, 'No.' And they also asked, 'Have you ever even seen a UFO?' And he said, 'No.' He had absolutely no UFO experiences whatsoever. Everything he knew about the subject, just as everything he knew probably about the comet or for that matter everything he knew about Christian theology, came via Applewhite.

"I pointed out how the UFO cults," Hopkins said, "such as this one, that has no knowledge of the UFO phenomenon whatsoever, and no personal experience, is essentially a situation of 'all beliefs and no miracles.' Whereas we investigators are looking at a phenomenon that is in effect 'all miracles and no beliefs.'"

Hopkins did, however, manage to salvage a little hope from the situation.

"I think that what it can do for us," he said, "is to perhaps let us people doing UFO research, people who've had UFO experiences, etc., take refuge in the richness of the human spirit and in the richness of our fellow human beings. We might keep our eyes at the sky just to see what's going on, but also realize that whatever is going on up there is alien to us and that down here, on our planet, is all the spiritual riches that any of us could ever want."

Just as the UFO and alien abduction phenomena remain mysteries that are still along way from being understood, so does the death of 39 cult members take its place among the many UFO-related mysteries that will continue to puzzle all those who seek a solution in real-world terms to things that most likely have their origin in worlds very different from our own.

Were the cult members the first martyrs to a new Space Age religion? Are they deluded victims of the religious madness of yet another lunatic cult leader? Perhaps that answer can only come after the passage of time, after we see what the New Millennium actually does bring in the way of apocalypse or business-as-usual, after more genuine, level-headed research into UFOs and the people who witness them.

Above all, we need to approach the search for the truth with a great deal more patience than the members of Heaven's Gate, who were so tragically already certain they had found the answer.

Chapter Six
The Meaning Of Prophecy

When a person makes the decision to try and read the prophets of the Bible in order to understand how the end will come, he usually comes away feeling a bit confused. This is because the Bible often doesn't speak plainly about the end, but rather couches much of its prophecy in symbolism. I think it is written that way for a couple of reasons.

First of all, if the details were simply spelled out, and such things as the name of the Antichrist were given openly and without recourse to a hidden language, then who in their right mind would stand back and just let those prophecies be fulfilled? Who could passively watch while someone with a predetermined name first took action to enslave the world, then led it to its destruction?

Most people are familiar with the notion that the Bible deals with, among many other things, the so-called "End of the World." That understanding of the Bible is derived from its numerous books of prophecy, from both the Old and New Testaments. The idea that the end was created with the beginning is one of those very tricky elements of faith that typically eludes a normal understanding of time. This chapter will deal with what is implied when prophecies made over two thousand years ago begin to be fulfilled in our own time.

FREE WILL VERSUS PREDESTINATION

The idea that the future can be accurately foretold creates a problem for people who believe completely in the idea of Free Will. If a prophesied event must be assumed to come true, there is logically no way to prevent that from happening. No amount of human effort could overcome the force in time that "makes" the prophecy come true, therefore the notion of Free Will becomes a useless and ineffectual way of viewing reality.

Take for instance the universally held Christian belief that Jesus Christ is the Messiah foretold by the prophets of the Old Testament. Everything from his birth in Bethlehem by his Virgin Mother to his eventual crucifixion and resurrection are said to have been predicted by everyone from Moses to Isaiah to the Psalms of King David.

If indeed Christ was predestined to fulfill all those ancient scriptures, and there is no way that he could not fulfill them, it cannot truly be said that he had Free Will. Once that point is conceded, the next thing that suggests itself is the idea that Christ walked through the events and settings of the story of the Gospel able only to carry out the will of his Heavenly Father, while everyone else in that landscape was free to act as they chose. The conflict becomes obvious, and creates an alarming either/or situation. Either Christ had Free Will, or no one did.

The Apostle Paul quite frankly states his own personal belief in the idea of predestination, claiming that those who eventually enter heaven were "predestined" to do so. In Romans 8:29, he wrote, "For those whom he foreknew, he also predestined to be conformed to the image of his Son, in order that he might be the first-born among many brethren. And those whom he predestined, he also called; and those whom he called he also justified; and those whom he justified he also glorified."

And later, in the Book of Revelation, reference is made to the Book of the Lamb, which lists the names of all those who will enter heaven, names inscribed from before the world was even created. It seems the cards are stacked before we even start playing the game, doesn't it?

For many people, those ideas create a sense that something less than fair play is happening here, and that only moral robots are worthy of salvation. Perhaps the only adequate answer to that lies in the fact that we as mortals simply don't understand the nature of time since we are constantly forced to perceive it from within, in the continual confusion of the material world. Neither do we understand judgment in that context, simply because the mortal mind is inadequate beyond a certain childlike understanding that it will all make perfect sense some day. Just like the problem of evil, predestination is an imponderably difficult thing to wrap our brains around.

THE PROPHETS OF THE BIBLE

Many people think the prophecies of the Bible come mostly at the end, in the Book of Revelation. However, the God of the Bible begins to prophesy in the very first book, Genesis.

After the Fall of Adam and Eve in the Garden of Eden, the Lord begins to hand out punishments. To the serpent, he says, "I will put enmity between you and the woman, and between your seed and her seed, he shall bruise your head and you shall bruise his heel." (Genesis 3:15).

This has been widely interpreted as predicting the coming of Christ many thousands of years later. While Satan would manage to bruise the heel of Jesus, Jesus would, by his resurrection, inflict more damage on the serpent's head.

God also prophesies what would be the future plight of mankind. To Eve, he says, "I will greatly multiply your pain in childbearing; in pain shall you bring forth children, yet your desire shall be for your husband, and he shall rule over you."

To Adam, he says, "Because you have listened to the voice of your wife, and have eaten of the tree of which I commanded you, 'You shall not eat of it,' cursed is the ground because of you, in toil shall you eat of it all the days of your life, . . . In the sweat of your face you shall eat bread, till you return to the ground, for out of it you were taken; you are dust, and to dust you shall return." (Genesis 3: 16-19).

There, in a few skillfully written broad strokes, the Lord prophesies what was to become the human condition, which has been just as he describes ever since. From that initial reckoning in the dim, dark days of mankind's past, a crucial chain of events began with a prophecy, and that same chain will be ended by the fulfillment of prophecies that came later.

THE USE OF SYMBOLISM IN BIBLICAL PROPHECY

When a person makes the decision to try and read the prophets of the Bible in order to understand how the end will come, he usually comes away feeling a bit confused. This is because the Bible often doesn't speak plainly about the end, but rather couches much of its prophecy in symbolism. I think it is written that way for a couple of reasons.

First of all, if the details were simply spelled out, and such things as the name of the Antichrist were given openly and without recourse to a hidden language, then who in their right mind would stand back and just let those prophecies be fulfilled? Who could passively watch while someone with a predetermined name first took action to enslave the world, then led it to its destruction?

So instead of naming names, as with the Antichrist, for example, we are given the following vagaries instead.

"Also it [the Antichrist] causes all, both small and great, both rich and poor, both free and slave, to be marked on the right hand or on the forehead, so that no one can buy or sell unless he has the mark, that is, the name of the beast or the number of its name. This calls for wisdom: let him who has understanding reckon the number of the beast, for it is a human number, its number is six hundred and sixty-six." (Revelation 13: 16-18).

For the sake of background, there is today a widely accepted understanding of those verses that argues that the actual method for implementing such a system of marking individuals already exists. Recent technology has made it possible to implant beneath a person's skin a transponder that could be scanned like a loaf of bread at the grocery store checkout and would include all kinds of relevant factual data about that person. The implanted transponder could even function as a miniature credit card that would track one's expenditures, hence the part about not being able to buy or sell without one.

But the point is that the Book of Revelation doesn't simply say "transponders," but speaks in a rich symbolic language instead. As with most prophecies that come to be at least partially fulfilled, as is the case with the one under discussion here, we understand the fulfillment more as a matter of hindsight than by actually understanding what it's saying about the future. Now that we know that transponders and various other technological methods exist, the fulfillment becomes comprehensible looking back in time, not forward. However much we may believe in the prophets, it is usually not possible to know how the symbols will come to fruition before they actually do.

NOSTRADAMUS AND THE NEED TO CONCEAL

The medieval French seer Nostradamus was no stranger to symbolism. He often rendered things obscure when it would have been much easier to simply spell them out in plain language. His problem was a little different, though. He was born a Jew, as is true of all the Biblical prophets, but he lived in the time of the Inquisition, when simply being Jewish was reason enough to be tortured and killed as a blasphemer, and his strange ability to see the future could easily be interpreted as witchcraft and black magic, which could also prove fatal in those times.

So Nostradamus chose instead to play games with words, including writing most of his prophecies as short, four line poems, called "quatrains," that even rhyme in their original language. He also threw in some anagrams, most of which have still not been completely deciphered, as well as occasional foreign words when it suited his fancy.

Much has been made of the fact that he was able to point the finger at Adolph Hitler, centuries before that maniac's rise to power, by calling him by the name of a river that runs through Germany called "Hister," actually an ancient name for the Danube River.

It has been said that "Hister" also suggests the Greek word for "hysteria," which may be an indirect reference to the dictator's disturbed mental state. But again, this sort of detailed understanding has come only through hindsight, by looking back at symbols that now make a great deal more sense than they could have when Nostradamus first wrote them down.

THE PROPHETS ARE IMPERFECT

While a great deal of this book will be taken up with the prophecies of the Bible and Nostradamus, it is important to say at the outset that the prophets and their prophecies are admittedly imperfect. The Apostle Paul says as much in Romans 12:6 when he writes, "Having gifts that differ according to the grace given to us, let us use them: if prophecy, in proportion to our faith." Since prophecy, even though it may come directly from the mouth of God, is still a human effort, the usual imperfections of humankind also play a large part in what finally gets written down for later generations to ponder.

A certain amount of tolerance is required here. St. Paul also says in Second Corinthians 5:13 that a degree of craziness may even enter the picture. "For if we are beside ourselves," he wrote, "it is for God; if we are in our right mind, it is for you." The phrase "beside ourselves" is a pretty accurate description of schizophrenia when it comes down to it. Schizophrenia is a word meaning "the divided self," as one would have to be to stand "beside" one's self.

Another way to approach the idea of prophecy as imperfect is to study some recent fulfillment's of predictions made by Nostradamus.

The September 11, 2001, terrorist attack on the World Trade Center was quite publicly stated to have been a fulfillment of the Nostradamus prophecy numbered Century VI, Quatrain 97, which reads:

"The sky will burn at forty-five degrees, Fire approaches the great New City. Immediately a huge scattered flame leaps up when they want to have proof of the Normans." (Translation by Erika Cheetham.)

As was said at the time, Nostradamus' prophecy is only a partial success. While it quite clearly names New York City as the location and offers a nearly exact visual description of what the world actually saw over and over again on the videotape taken at the time, "Immediately, a scattered flame leaps up," it also fails on a couple of points. New York City is not located at the 45th parallel but at the 48th instead. Also, the reference to wanting "proof of the Normans," which is often interpreted as referring to France, seems to make no logical sense at all in this context.

There is another near-miss in Nostradamus' work that may also apply here: the famous "1999 prophecy" found in Century X, Quatrain 72. The quatrain reads as follows:

"In the year 1999, and seven months, from the sky will come the great King of Terror. He will bring to life the great king of the Mongols. Before and afterward, war reigns happily." (Translation by Erika Cheetham.)

In July of 1999, John F. Kennedy, Jr. and his wife died in a plane crash, making headlines throughout the world, but it would be ludicrous to conclude that he qualified as the "great King of Terror" from the sky. It seems much more logical to infer that Nostradamus was again predicting the September 11 attack, but that he simply got the year wrong—a year before the millennium instead of a year after. It is not such a stretch to acknowledge that occasionally major components of a prophecy get a little garbled both by the elusive nature of time as well as by the human factor in the prophetic process.

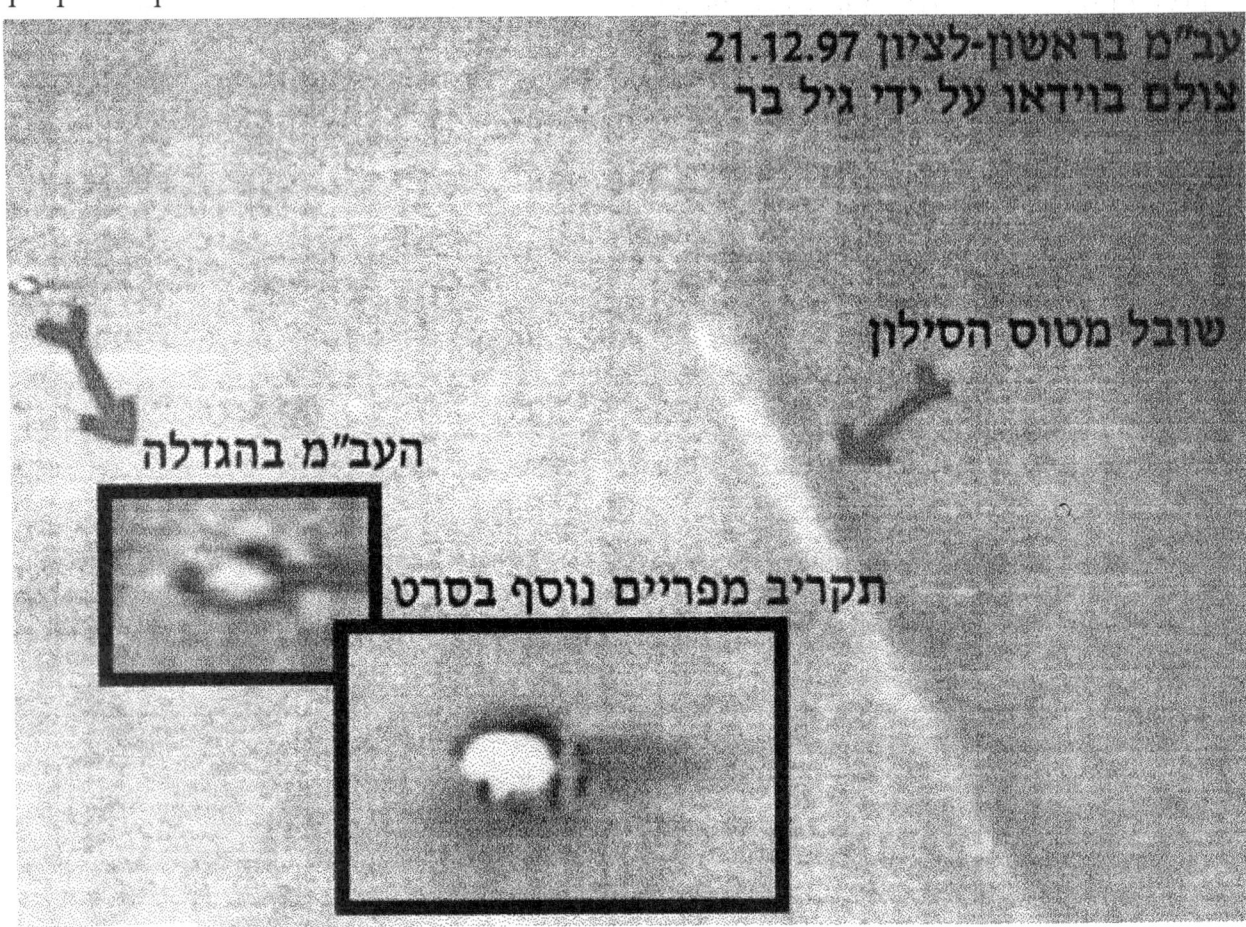

In a front page story UFO is chased by military plane over Israel.

Chapter Seven
Gary Stearman And Predictions From The Bible

"The Twin Towers of the World Trade Center are an edifice of global banking, global merchandise, controlled by European and American banking interests. And these interests are the offspring of the Crusaders, the wealthy leaders of Europe in the Middle Ages. So it's an ancient battle brought right up to the present day."

Gary Stearman is a researcher and writer for Dr. J.R. Church's television ministry Prophecy In The News. As the name implies, the ministry is focused on Biblical prophecy as it is fulfilled by current news events. The ministry is based in Oklahoma City, Oklahoma, and publishes a monthly magazine along with a weekly television program that is seen by satellite and on cable throughout the United States.

Stearman said that he came to the Bible by a nonstandard route. When he grew bored with his studies at university in engineering, he switched his major to psychology, which he pursued about halfway through a masters degree. However, it was his minors in linguistics, creative writing and literature that would later come to serve him best. He took a job as a writer and supervisor of commercial publications at Beech Aircraft Company.

"But essentially my university work was creative writing, history, and English, specifically Shakespearian studies," Stearman said. "I even took Greek. I feel in retrospect that the Lord was kind of leading me toward Bible study. It was not until after I graduated and had been in the corporate world for several years that I received Christ at the age of thirty-two. I was taken completely by surprise, having never been raised in a Biblical environment. I was utterly overwhelmed by the Bible. From the first minute that I received Christ, I began to study.

"I was in comparative Shakespearian studies," he continued, "which involved studying the history of language, linguistic comparisons. I discovered that all of that work transferred itself into Bible study. And the more I studied, the more I discovered that scripture is indeed divinely inspired, divinely ordained, and controlled in every aspect by God."

Stearman said that he has collected a large library of two or three thousand volumes on the Bible and has spent the last thirty years totally immersed in the subject. In 1983, he founded a church in Oklahoma City called "Grace Fellowship." He was working as a freelance scriptural writer when he met J.R. Church, the founder of Prophecy In The

Gary Stearman

News, at a lecture Church was giving in 1987. The two men talked at length about Biblical prophecy, with Stearman offering some discoveries of his own.

"It became very obvious to both of us," Stearman recalled, "that I could be of help to him as a researcher. So anyway, that's kind of a strange bio. I started out in commercial business and the Lord took me into pastoral work and Christian writing."

ISRAEL'S MODERN REBIRTH

One of the fundamental bricks that modern understanding of Biblical prophecy is built of has to do with the rebirth of Israel as a nation in the 20th Century. Without a State of Israel to provide a staging ground for the predicted events to center around, there might not be any real credibility owed to the many prophets of the Bible. Stearman said that beginning in the early 1830s, several scholars began to look forward to the establishment of a new Israel, and the Zionist movement that sprang up soon afterward set the wheels in motion for just such an event.

"A number of men," Stearman said, "taught that Israel would soon be established as a nation, and when it was, it would be a fulfillment of prophecy. Of course that happened in 1948. Those who have observed this have all been in agreement that the major fulfillment of Bible prophecy in the 20th Century is the establishment of the State of Israel."

And what is the scriptural basis for that belief?

"There are just a number of scriptures," Stearman replied. "Of course, Ezekiel Chapters 36 and 37 speak of the nations coming together in a particular way in which a global world order would be established. The prophet Jeremiah speaks of the re-gathering of Israel. In Jeremiah 31:31, 'Behold the days come, saith the Lord, that I will make a new covenant with the House of Israel and the House of Judah.' And all of this is set in the context of Israel being re-gathered back into the land in the latter days.

"I suppose there must be over one hundred major scriptural passages that speak of Israel being re-gathered and established as a nation in the latter days. And along with that establishment, prophecy says consistently that Israel would suffer opposition of every sort from the moment it became a modern state until the return of Jesus to this world. Israel would struggle against all odds for its very existence. Which we see today of course."

THE EVENTS OF SEPTEMBER 11, 2001

One question I was eager to ask Stearman concerned just how the terrorist attack of September 11, 2001, fit into the general scheme of prophecy.

"Well," Stearman began, "if you look at the parties that are contesting each other, you discover that the real battle began in the Middle Ages when the Crusaders and the forces of Islam battled over the Holy City. For a few years, the Crusaders actually captured Jerusalem until they were run out by the forces of Saladin approaching the 13th Century. When that happened, the Crusaders retreated for a while and the forces of Islam actually began to move into what had been the territory of Western Civilization. If you examine the current Islamic drive for jihad, you discover it's a battle that's been fought back and forth across European soil since 1100 or so. It's an ancient battle—the Crusaders versus the Islamics." Stearman pointed out that the terrorist Osama bin Laden still uses the term "Crusaders."

"In fact, you will hear Osama bin Laden often referring to the forces of the West as the 'Crusaders,'" Stearman said. "They do not regard the battle as having been dropped in any way. For them, it's still an open, raging battle. They see the West, that is Europe and America, as a force that must be eliminated before Islam can rise to its full glory.

"So when they attacked the World Trade Center, they were attacking essentially the centerpiece of the Crusader forces," he continued. "The Twin Towers of the World Trade Center are an edifice of global banking, global merchandise, controlled by European and American banking interests. And these interests are the offspring of the Crusaders, the wealthy leaders of Europe in the Middle Ages. So it's an ancient battle brought right up to the present day."

Stearman went on to explain further.

"There are two things that Islam hates," he said. "They hate the Western merchant-trader and global banking. And they also hate what they call 'Zionism'. They're taking that word directly out of the Bible. Zion is the piece of real estate known as the Temple Mount in Jerusalem. And the Zionist movement, which began really seriously in 1897 and continues to this day, is a movement which desires to center the life of Israel around the Temple Mount, which has been, and still is, the most contested piece of real estate on the face of the Earth.

"Because of our general financial aid to Israel, the West is seen as supporting Zionism. And so the twofold hatred of the modern Islamics movement is against

Western business, finance and also against Zionism, which is said to be holding hands with Western business interests."

Stearman also quoted a passage from Isaiah that now seems eerily prescient.

"In Isaiah 30, verse 25, there is a word from the Lord," he said, "on the destruction of the enemies of Israel. The verse says, 'And there shall be upon every high mountain, and upon every high hill, rivers and streams of water, in the day of great slaughter, when the towers fall.' And this has been quoted by a number of people recently as possibly referring to the Twin Towers, and it may.

"Generically, I think it refers to the towers of global power. The great skyscrapers, you know, and the accumulation of power in the West. And then the next verse says, 'Moreover the light of the moon shall be as the light of the sun, and the light of the sun shall be sevenfold, and so forth, which is speaking of the great and terrible day of the Lord. It puts the falling towers in the same context as the day of the Lord. So I think that's a fascinating prophecy."

WAS GLOBAL WARMING PREDICTED IN THE BIBLE?

When I asked Stearman for any specific predictions about the near future that he could offer, he referred back to the prophecy he had just been quoting.

"I think number one," he said, "the thing that people need to look for, particularly in the light of that prophecy I just read in Isaiah 30:26, where it talks about the variability of the light of the sun and moon—over and over again in scripture, we see that there is going to be a cataclysmic variability in the sun. At one point, it apparently causes people to seek shade because the sun is burning their skin, indicating that the light of the sun is seven times brighter than usual. In another place, it's so dark that men can't find their way around for want of light.

"So I think we can look for solar, terrestrial disturbances," he said. "Now it's fascinating that in the last year, we have seen exactly this. The number of magnetic storms on the sun has reached record levels in the year 2001, and is continuing right on to the present. And it's affecting the weather on Earth and possibly the other planets. By the way, this is available on public record.

The New York Times and *The New York Post*, for example, have noted that not only is the Earth's climate warming up, but also the climate of Mars is warming up, and they're noticing that the Martian polar cap is disappearing at a rapid rate. And the only explanation for this that they've been able to come up with is that the sun is getting hotter. So global warming, which people are worried about, is perhaps not caused by manmade pollutants, but may be an extraterrestrial event.

"Now with these solar magnetic flares, these magnetic storms, come violent changes in the weather. A lot of people have been predicting abnormally large hurricanes, tornados, unusual and out of place weather fronts, etc., and we're beginning to observe those. So in terms of what the Bible predicts in the immediate future, wild excursions in the weather, perhaps variability in the sun and solar storms, I think that's something we can definitely be on the lookout for."

Stearman said that the Day of the Lord is described by some of the prophets of the Bible as "a day of darkness" or a "a day of gloominess," which may be characterized by strange instabilities in the weather the likes that have never been seen before. He also quoted Isaiah 24, verses 19 and 20: "The Earth is utterly broken down, the Earth is rent asunder, the Earth is shaken violently, the Earth shall stagger like a drunken man . . . . and the transgressions thereof shall be heavy upon it, and it shall fall and not rise again."

"So with the upcoming tribulation," he concluded, "I look for geomagnetic solar terrestrial difficulty, perhaps abnormally warm weather in Canada and abnormally cold weather in the tropics—all sorts of upheavals that cause mankind to become very afraid."

WHY IS SUCH HARSH JUDGMENT NECESSARY?

At one point, I broached the question that bothers many people who believe in the fulfillment of apocalyptic prophecies, no matter the source. Why is such harsh judgment necessary to God's plan for mankind?

"Why does the tribulation feature such horrors for the planet Earth?" Stearman asked, echoing my question. "Why such harsh judgment? Going back to the Old Testament, all of the Old Testament prophets, including Moses, speak of a humanity which has fallen to such severe depths of apostasy that it has to be judged severely. The story of the Bible, in my opinion, is the story of God giving humanity a number of chances to make the right choices, but in every case humanity makes the wrong choice and always opts for power and wealth over godliness. This is basically the prophetic story of the Bible.

"And so by the time you come through the age of the great rulers," he went on, "the Caesars in the days of Jesus, by the time you come through the era of the churches to the present day, you have the world turning progressively away from God and toward pleasure and paganism. And God says he must judge this. That judgment is based upon covenantal promises that he made in the Old Testament. For example, to Abraham he made a promise. To Moses he made a promise. To the kings of Israel, beginning with King David, he made promises concerning the Kingdom. And those promises all have to be worked out.

"And in order for them to be worked out, the powers of the Earth must be overthrown. So when you get to the tribulation period, the first thing you see is the Antichrist moving forward into a final position of control of a world government. You see war, famine, you see the saints of God persecuted, and you see a global rule set up under ten kings.

"A third of the Earth is destroyed," he continued, "one third of the salt water is destroyed, one third of the fresh water is destroyed, one third of the heavens are destroyed. The sun is made dark. A great hole or cave is opened in the ground which allows demon spirits to come out and torment humans. And they manage to kill one third of the population of the Earth, according to Revelation, and that of course would amount to two billion people given the present population."

As if that weren't mind-boggling enough, there is more, according to Stearman and his interpretations.

"Then there is a second wave of difficulties," he explained. "There is another world war. Men are excoriated with various kinds of insults that eat their flesh, and with sores. All of the sea life in the salt water is utterly destroyed, followed by another cataclysm in the bowl judgments in which all the fresh water is made foul. The heat of the sun is increased sevenfold, followed by a blackout of the sun. And you can just go on and on this way. What you end up with is an amazing picture of God's righteous judgment.

"That is to say," Stearman said, "that his judgments are not arbitrary. They follow a specific pattern, and that pattern was set forth back in the days of the Exodus, when the ten plagues were meted out upon the Egyptians under Moses. Those plagues freed the Israelites to move to the Promised Land. Likewise, in the latter days, the plagues of Revelation will free the Israelites once again to move into the Kingdom. So this is judgment with a purpose."

JUDGMENT VERSUS CHASTENING

Next I asked Stearman if he felt that the terrorist attack of September 11 or the current problems Israel is having fit into the patterns of judgment we were discussing. His answer was very interesting.

"There's a difference," he said, "between judgment and chastening. I believe that you see in the Bible that the nations, the pagan forces of the Earth, are judged. But Israel is chastened. That is to say, Israel is cleansed. And the purpose of the tribulation, by the way, is ultimately to restore Israel to the land. That's something that must never be forgotten."

Stearman went on to say that God has promised three reasons for the tribulation, giving chapter and verse, which seems to come very easily to him.

"Number one," he began, "to make an end of wickedness, Isaiah 13:9. Number two, to bring about a worldwide revival, Revelation 7:1. And number three, to break the power of the holy people, as in Daniel 12:5-7. The holy people are Israel, who have been very proudly subsisting as a nation in their own right. God's ultimate purpose is to break their self-confidence and bring them into godly submission to his rule. So that is chastening, as opposed to judgment with a vengeance, which is meted out on the nations."

DAMASCUS AND THE PEACE PROCESS

And what prophecies apply to the so-called Middle East "peace process"? Again, Stearman had a ready answer.

"I always point people to the 17th chapter of Isaiah," he said, "which sets up a situation we may see fulfilled in the very near future. It's the famous prophecy about the burden of Damascus. 'Behold, Damascus is taken away from being a city, and shall be a ruinous heap.' And this chapter goes on to describe how Damascus will be wiped out in a 24-hour period. Now this prophecy has never been fulfilled because Damascus is the world's oldest continuously occupied city. It's well over 4,000 years old, and it's always prospered.

"But this prophecy takes place in the context of re-gathered Israel," he continued. "And there is a war that comes, and in Isaiah 17:4, in the context of the destruction of Damascus, it says, 'And in that day, it shall come to pass that the glory of Jacob shall be made thin, and the fatness of his flesh shall wax lean.' In other words, yes, the Lord will judge the nations.

"Right now virtually everyone regards the Syrians as perhaps the number one enemy of Israel, in spite of a lot of other highly advertised enemies, like Osama bin Laden and Saddam Hussein and so forth. But [Syrian leader] Bashar al Assad has a larger army and heavier armaments than just about anybody in the area, and he has the intention to use them. I'm sure the Syrians are going to be destroyed in an upcoming war, but I'm also sure that the glory of Jacob 'shall be made thin.' In other words, it looks like at that time that Israel's going to suffer some collateral damage of some sort. That's exactly what's predicted for the Tribulation. They'll have to run for their lives for a short time until they are saved."

Stearman gave more details on the Syrian military buildup.

"This prophecy of Isaiah 17 is one that I would watch," he said, "because the Syrians are arming themselves to the hilt with medium range ballistic missiles with chemical and biological warheads. Some people say they already have nuclear warheads and they have the largest supply of Russian arms in the Middle East. They are electronically quite well advanced. They have the tools of modern warfare.

"Their leader, Bashar al Assad, is a very intelligent man. He speaks fluent English, was educated in the West, and is totally dedicated to wiping out, as he calls it, 'The Zionist Entity,' which is their name for Israel. And so Isaiah 17 really is a key prophetic chapter. I would be looking for a major war in the Middle East, and one of the prominent features of that war is the complete flattening of Damascus. The final verse in Isaiah 17 says that, 'Behold, at evening tide, trouble, and before the morning, he is not.' In other words, within a few hours Damascus will be totally flattened. And that really sounds nuclear to me."

A WARNING IN THE PRESENT TENSE

Stearman offered a final warning, one that he feels even the secular mind should understand and take to heart.

"If I wanted to point the secular mind to something," he said, "that is absolutely present tense and very powerful, I would point to Zecheriah 12, the burden of the Lord for Israel. 'Sayeth the Lord, which stretches forth the heavens, which lays the foundations of the Earth and formed the spirit of man within him, 'Lo, I am about to make Jerusalem a cup of trembling,' or a cup of poison it reads in Hebrew, 'unto all people round about when they shall be in siege both against Judah and Jerusalem.'

"Well, they are in siege now," Stearman said. "The PLO and the Arab brotherhood have a siege against Judah and Jerusalem. 'And in that day I shall make Jerusalem a burdensome stone for all people.' That has already come to pass right now. 'All that burden themselves with it shall be cut in pieces. So all people of the Earth shall be gathered against it.' That's happened right now."

Stearman next quoted from Isaiah, the sixth verse.

"The very next prophecy that comes out of that," he explained, "is 'In that day will I make the governors of Judah like a hearth of fire among the wood, and like a torch of fire in a sheave, and they shall devour all of the people roundabout, on the right hand and on the left. And Jerusalem shall be inhabited again in her own place, even in Jerusalem.' So you have a very clear prophecy here, that the nations will be in siege against Jerusalem, that in that day the governors of Judah will be like a hearth of fire among the wood. In other words, they're going to set fire to their enemies. Which again has a very nuclear ring to it."

So Israel will eventually be victorious?

"Yes, but in the process," Stearman replied, "I think Israel goes through some precipitous times. War is never fun for either side. By the way, these 'governors of Judah' in verse six are the Hebrew word for 'secular leader.' We know this is a latter day prophecy because only since 1948 has Israel had secular leaders—Knesset [parliament] members. So this is specifically a prophecy that applies to our day."

Stearman offered one final prophecy, again about Israel and her enemies.

"We read in Psalm 83," he said, "that 'They have taken crafty counsel against thy people, and consulted against thy hidden ones. They have said, "Come, let us cut them off from being a nation, that the name of Israel may be no more in remembrance," for they have consulted together with one consent.' In other words, all of the descendants of Israel's traditional enemies are gathered together to cut Israel off from being a nation. We have that in Psalm 83. And 1983 just happens to be the year that Yassir Arafat reformed the PLO after it was dissolved in 1982. And from that day to this, there has been a continuous assault on Israel. So I believe there are a number of present, active prophecies in the Bible."

Chapter Eight
UFOs and the Military—Doomsday Scenario?

"I would think that right on top of that list of problems is the release of atomic energy through the detonation of atomic bombs. You must remember that the whole modern UFO wave started when we were developing and exploding the first atomic bomb.

"I honestly think, and this is pure speculation, but I really think the message is, 'Let's do away with nuclear weapons. Don't play with these nuclear weapons, because we're going to destroy ourselves with it.' I think they mean to send some kind of message like that. Because all they did was disable the missiles. I think they probably had the capability of doing a lot more, and that's all they did."

Since the first days of the modern UFO era, there have been so many sightings close to nuclear installations that it has become an undeniable fact that, whoever the UFO occupants turn out to be, they have an obvious interest in the atomic weapons of both sides. Even after the end of the Cold War, they still seem to be sending us a message about the mind-boggling dangers involved in the merest contemplation of the use of our nuclear weapons.

Is that the beginnings of a possible scenario of future doom? Would we take up arms and shoot the nukes at an invading army of UFOs, something similar to the Battle of Armageddon in the Book of Revelation? Or might the aliens somehow pit us against some foreign enemy against whom we unleashed our nuclear arsenal unwittingly? Such nightmares remain in the realm of the possible.

INCIDENT IN MONTANA

An incident occurred in Montana in 1967 that is a classic example of the aliens' knowledge of and interest in our nuclear capabilities. Former Air Force First Lieutenant Robert Salas was on missile duty as deputy missile crew commander on the night of March 16 at a Minuteman Missile Launch Control Facility sixty feet underground when something happened that changed his view of reality forever.

"I had a commander," Salas told me in an interview in 1996, "and we alternated sleep sessions. So he was asleep in the early morning hours when I got a call from one of my security guards upstairs. He said he and the other guards up there had been observing lights flying over the facility. They were not airplanes. And I think he even used the term 'UFOs,' but I kind of disregarded it. I wasn't a staunch believer then. And then about five minutes later he calls back, and this time he's really frightened. Very anxious. He says there's a UFO hovering right beside the front gate and it's glowing red. It was just a very reddish light.

"After I hung up with the guard," he continued, "I woke up my commander and was telling him about the phone calls. And as I told him, the missiles started shutting down. That is, they went 'No Go.' They couldn't be launched. This is very unusual, because we had nothing even remotely similar to missiles going 'No Go' like that without any reason. This was not just a power loss of the missiles, by the way. It was not that they lost electrical power at the sites. They actually just went into a condition where they couldn't be launched."

THE PROBLEM SPREADS

Meanwhile, something similar was happening at another nearby installation, Salas said.

"Well, we reported this to our Command Post," he said, "and they told us the that the same thing has happened at another site. And, sure enough, we talked to the other site's commander and he confirmed that, yes, all ten of his missiles had shut down. There were also UFOs sighted at the launch facilities where the missiles are actually located. They're dispersed throughout the countryside there, away from the launch control center. So we're looking at somewhere close to twenty missiles being disabled at the same time that UFOs are being observed by military personnel."

After Salas and his crew were relieved later that day and flown back to Malmstrom Air Force Base, they were debriefed by Air Force officials, including an officer from the Air Force Office of Special Investigation, who were just as surprised as Salas and the others were by what happened.

"There was no hint or indication that this was any kind of an Air Force exercise," Salas said. "And the squadron commander and his deputy and everyone I talked to when we got back was just as surprised and flabbergasted at what had happened. So this was not an Air Force exercise. It was a classified incident. We were not to talk to anybody about it. I was at the base for another three years and the incident was never discussed again. We were not debriefed about the investigation of it, and we couldn't even talk amongst ourselves about it."

SALAS TAKES ACTION ON HIS OWN

Salas said he decided to talk about what happened 28 years later when he read UFO researcher Timothy Good's book *Above Top Secret*. Good's book contained a report on the incident at the other installation that Salas had been in contact with that night.

Salas' next move was to send a Freedom of Information Act (FOIA) request to the Air Force.

"I didn't mention anything about UFOs," he said. "And they declassified the incident and sent me a historical abstract, a unit history, about the incident. So I did get copies of that. As a result of the FOIA requests, I also got copies of telegrams that went back and forth between the Air Force and the contractor. One of the telegrams said that this was of grave concern to the Air Force."

Salas also contacted a couple of employees of the Boeing Company who had been on the civilian contractor's investigating team.

"They verified that there was never a plausible explanation for this incident," he said.

Salas said that he has also contacted many of the other Air Force personnel involved in the Minuteman Missile incident and that they all confirm his version of events.

"In addition, we've got UFO reports that were made in *The Great Falls Tribune*," he said. "Reports were published in the *Tribune* that were made by civilians living in the area all the way from early February through the end of March, 1967. I've got copies. As a matter of fact, one of the reports was by a state patrolman."

RAYMOND FOWLER ENTERS THE PICTURE

Meanwhile, across the country, another drama was unfolding that was the result of the events that Salas had witnessed. World-renowned UFO researcher Raymond Fowler [for more background on Fowler, see Chapter Three] was working at the time on the production board for the Minuteman Missile program as an employee for GT Sylvania.

"We were switching equipment around in the launch facilities all the time," Fowler said. "At that time, I was responsible for keeping track of the equipment, and I documented not only our equipment but everybody else's equipment. So the people at the site were telling me about the incidents. I wanted to know more, so I went to the Boeing representative who was at GT Sylvania at the time. He was always interested in showing how much he could find out about certain things. He knew the assistant base manager out there in Montana, so I asked him about what had happened and he said he could find out for me."

The call the Boeing representative made turned out to be anything but routine.

"He called out there," Fowler continued, "and I was watching his face as he talked to the assistant base manager. And when he hung up, he said it was a 'hot potato' and I should never have asked him to ask that question. He was really upset that I'd even had him call about it."

But curiosity about the UFO-related incidents continued to gnaw at Fowler, and he went on digging for more information.

"That wasn't the only incident," he said. "There were a lot of incidents going on out there. One of them involved a launch control facility officer who was going through on-the-job training and was becoming acquainted with all the different contractors. He came to GT Sylvania and he was with a contract administrator from the program office. They came by my desk and the contract administrator said, 'That's Ray Fowler there. He believes in UFOs, ha ha.'

"And the officer said, 'Wait a minute,' and he stopped. Then he told me about an incident where UFOs appeared over the base and were affecting equipment in the launch control facilities that he was in."

FOWLER, HYNEK AND THE PRESS

Fowler later discussed that same incident with the late Dr. J. Allen Hynek, the Chief Consultant for the Air Force on UFO matters.

"He told me that not only did it affect the equipment at the launch control facility," Fowler said, "but two of the ships appeared to land. They sent out strike teams to the assumed landing site, and their communications were jammed. Some F-106s were scrambled, and their communications were jammed as well. The UFOs took off and couldn't be caught."

Soon Fowler's interest in the subject of UFOs nearly affected his career quite drastically.

"*The Christian Science Monitor* approached me and wanted to do an article on UFOs," he said. "I sat down with a reporter and went over the whole UFO problem. I started to mention, just in passing, some of the things that happened out at the

Minuteman sites. A few days later, it was headline news in **The Christian Science Monitor** in this country and abroad about the Minuteman Missiles being disrupted by UFOs. Well, the next day, I was in my office and a friend of mine came in and said he was in the industrial manager's office and overheard a conversation with a Colonel William Coleman and the industrial manager of Sylvania. He sort of eavesdropped on the conversation and said, 'Sounds like you might be in trouble because the Air Force is going to send a letter of displeasure to your files.'

"The next day I was called into the office," Fowler went on, "and I was brought to someone who was just about to become the Vice-President and General Manager of Sylvania. They sort of read me the riot act and said that unless I could indicate that I found out this information from sources other than Sylvania, I could be in trouble. I could lose my security clearance and everything. So I told them that Dr. Hynek had supplied some information to me and that some of this information was in the public domain and so forth. And it ended up that nothing was done. But I was given a stern warning not to report anything. Also, the individual who was supplying me the most information told me that he couldn't supply me with anymore because their telephones were monitored periodically and someone in intelligence there had caught our conversation. And he was told not to talk about it anymore."

THE NEED FOR SECRECY

Fowler said he understands the need for secrecy.

"Suppose Russia had some type of satellite or something that could send EMP [electromagnetic phenomenon] signals that could jam Minuteman and so forth," he said. "Information like that would be highly classified. You could call it a cover-up, but I think it would be covering up for the sake of national security. Now, you have a machine-like object and you don't know what it is or where it comes from. It has the ability to jam not only equipment in a Minuteman, but can also jam interceptors and strike team's radios and so forth—that's considered a threat to national security. You have the nation's primary weapons systems being compromised. So I can see that information like that would be highly classified."

Salas also explained his own viewpoint regarding the secrecy maintained about the incident.

"These weapons went down in a 'No Go' condition," he said, "and they were down for a good period of time, close to a day. That affected our national retaliatory strike capability. We lost that ability for that amount of time, and certainly it impacted our national security."

But Salas is still not happy with the Air Force's refusal to tell the public the truth.

"In 1969, the Air Force issued a letter," he said. "It's a statement saying that no UFO incident—as a result of both their investigations under Blue Book and by the Condon Committee—no reported UFO incident ever affected national security. That's practically a verbatim quote. This was in 1969, and my incident happened in 1967. So the Air Force blatantly misrepresented the facts there as far as I'm concerned. They're deliberately covering this thing up. This was a major incident, and I've got the correspondence where SAC headquarters say, 'This was of very grave concern to this headquarters.'"

Salas said that this was not the attitude he had back in 1967.

"Then I was just following orders," he said. "This was classified and I didn't reveal anything. I basically put it out of my mind, or tried to. But now what I'm concerned about is that the government is holding this classified and lying about it even though this is something of great public interest. If these things are extraterrestrial—and I don't see how we can draw any other conclusion—then that fact alone is of general interest to the public. The reason I'm talking about it now is because I think the government should be forthcoming about what they know about UFOs in general.

"We've got probably a small group of individuals in government," Salas went on, "who are controlling this information. And who the heck knows what they're doing with it? Let's just speculate, for example, that they have gotten hold of some kind of alien technology. Do we want just a small group of people to have that technology? And do with it what they might or even communicate with extraterrestrials for the rest of us without our knowledge? This country's supposed to be based on the power of the people to have input into government actions, and instead we've got some mavericks in the government that have got this information. And who the heck knows what they're using it for? That's what I'm concerned about. It's a real concern about preserving democracy."

What about the idea that the government's releasing UFO information would cause a panic similar to the 1937 broadcast by Orson Welles of *The War of the Worlds*?

Salas replied by saying, "The Orson Welles thing was a broadcast that said we were under attack by Martians. To me, this would be completely different. Because we're not under attack and we know we're not under attack. So I don't think there would be that kind of reaction, for one. Number two, you know, you've got to trust the public as a whole not to panic over something like this. I just don't buy that argument."

WHY THE ALIEN INTEREST IN OUR NUKES?

Why do the aliens take this apparent interest in our nuclear facilities to begin with? Both Salas and Fowler had ready answers. We'll let Fowler go first.

"It all goes back to what abductees are being told," he said. "That there's a symbiotic relationship between them and us. And if pollution, whether it be radiation or other types of pollution, is affecting life forms here, then somehow or other it affects them as well. So I would think that if that's true, what the abductees are being told—that mankind is going to become sterile and other life forms are going to become sterile, and that what they're doing with the cattle mutilations and abductions are directly related to this problem—I would think that right on top of that list of problems is the release of atomic energy through the detonation of atomic bombs. You must remember that the whole modern UFO wave started when we were developing and exploding the first atomic bomb."

Salas spoke along similar lines.

"I honestly think, and this is pure speculation, " he said, "but I really think the message is, 'Let's do away with nuclear weapons. Don't play with these nuclear weapons, because we're going to destroy ourselves with it.' I think they mean to send some kind of message like that. Because all they did was disable the missiles. I think they probably had the capability of doing a lot more, and that's all they did."

Perhaps Salas is right in saying we were spared something much worse that night in Montana in 1967. We can only hope that the "mercy" that was shown by the aliens is understood and appreciated by that small group Salas alludes to who so jealously guard the power to think and act for all of us.

A CHECKLIST OF OTHER INCIDENTS

Over the course of the years he spent working at GTE (which at the time was called GT Sylvania), as well as during the many years since, when he devoted himself to UFO research full-time, Raymond Fowler has had access to information about numerous incidents similar to the events at the Montana Minuteman Missile launch control facility in 1967. He therefore had a few more stories to tell, which are included here for the sake of demonstrating how common UFO encounters close to our nuclear facilities really are.

"I've talked to some people who claimed that missiles were re-targeted after some of these events had taken place out there," he said. "I think that [UFO researcher] Linda Moulton-Howe's brother was stationed out there in one of these UFO flaps and he claimed the same thing—that one of the missiles in a silo had its targeting interfered with and the whole thing was re-targeted. In fact, he said there was a UFO as big as a football field and the strike team wouldn't go near it when they were asked to. They actually disobeyed orders. And they said, 'If you want to approach this thing, send someone else. We aren't going to go near it.'

"At the time," Fowler continued, "they also sent fighters in. And when the fighters came online, the object just blinked out. The fighters circled around and started to run out of fuel on the way and then the lights came on again."

Another incident more recently came to Fowler's attention.

"I was talking to a B-36 pilot the other day," he said, "and he told me that during the Suez Canal Crisis they were on alert. They had the B-36s on the runway, and they couldn't leave their planes, which were loaded with atomic weapons. Food was being brought out to them because they couldn't leave the aircraft. He said they were ready to use nuclear weapons if Russia interfered in the Suez Canal Crisis.

"As they were on the flight line," Fowler continued, "this thing as big as a football field appeared at the end of the runway and just sat there. And I'm wondering, if the B-36s had taken off, what would this thing have done?"

Still another incident involved the theft of nuclear materials.

"A lieutenant colonel who was stationed at Pease Air Force Base told me that he was told by another officer of high integrity," Fowler said, "that a nuclear warhead had actually been taken. And in order to open one of those silos—there are three combination locks, he said, and then you've got these really heavy, heavy covers. The strike team got the signal that something was there, but when they got there all the locks had been compromised and the thing was open. And a nuclear warhead was gone."

Fowler discussed yet another case he had heard about on NBC's Dateline program.

"They investigated a case in Russia where a UFO came in and hovered over a missile base and an adjoining village," he said. "They interviewed a lot of villagers who had seen it. They also interviewed the missile commander, and he said a countdown had been started when this huge disc-shaped object was seen standing on end over the base. The countdown only lasted a few seconds, but it was as if Moscow had sent the correct code and the two launch facility officers had turned the keys and sent this missile on its way to the United States. Then the object left and the countdown stopped. Electronics people came in and took all the equipment and examined it, and there was nothing wrong with it.

"So you have enough of these incidents," Fowler concluded, "to indicate that someone is interested in preserving posterity as far as atomic weapons are concerned. Someone who is saying, 'We can do this,' and who is maybe giving us a warning."

THE LORD AND HIS WEAPONS

Both Raymond Fowler and Robert Salas believe that the alien interest in our nuclear capabilities is a peaceful one, a gentle nudge in the direction of total nuclear disarmament. One would certainly hope they are correct in how they assess the motives of the aliens.

But it occurred to me some time after I did the interviews with both gentlemen that maybe a certain passage from the Book of Isaiah might also be relevant to the discussion.

Isaiah Chapter 13, beginning with verse 4, says, "Hark, a tumult on the mountains as of a great multitude, Hark, an uproar of kingdoms, of nations gathering together! The Lord of hosts is mustering a host for battle,

"They come from a distant land, from the end of the heavens, the Lord and the weapons of his indignation, to destroy the whole earth,

"Wail, for the day of the Lord is near; as destruction from the Almighty it will come! Therefore all hands will be feeble, and every man's heart will melt, and they will be dismayed. Pangs and agony will seize them; they will be in anguish like a woman in travail.

"They will look aghast at one another; their faces will be aflame. Behold, the day of the Lord comes, cruel, with wrath and fierce anger, to make the earth a desolation and to destroy its sinners from it."

If it is true, as Salas and Fowler believe, that the aliens can control and manipulate our nuclear weapons at will, is it such a stretch to believe that the aliens are merely biding their time until they are ready for mankind to unleash the horrors of nuclear war on each other? Many passages in the prophets of the Bible make statements that seem to refer to a future nuclear holocaust, as do some pertinent quatrains in Nostradamus.

While anyone would prefer to believe that a benevolent alien force will step in to prevent such a terrible turn of events, it is still too soon to sit back and relax on that account. The Lord may have something very different in mind.

This picture was taken in the village of Nuzidath.

Chapter Nine
Diane Tessman: An Inspired Voice From The Future

"I am a vibrant, breathing ball of life. I will be cleansed. I will be healed. I am too strong to die. Other balls out there in space did not have my luck. Most could not sustain sacred life at the level I do. A very high level of life, a great diversity of life, is mine. I am very proud. Some living worlds have been zapped by asteroids or gamma rays or what have you. Life stops abruptly. All life stops. I have been spared. My location in the galaxy is fortunate. The spring is coming, when I do my magic as only I can.
"Join me then as you have never joined me before. Our spirits will entwine. You will heal me. I will heal you."

Diane Tessman can succinctly and best be described as a prophetess of the New Age. Her vision of the future is probably one of the most optimistic you will find in this book, and one cannot help but hope that hers is the correct one.

Tessman said that her spiritual journey began approximately twenty years ago. After working as a schoolteacher for more than a decade, she was led by way of a series of odd coincidences to discover an ability to "channel," or to receive prophetic messages from somewhere in the spiritual realm.

"My main contact is Tibus," Tessman said, "who calls himself a voice from Earth's future. I felt that I had a UFO experience with him when I was a child. A very positive experience—nothing frightening and no medical experiments. But a visitation nevertheless. I remembered it while in hypnosis. I don't remember it consciously. But for almost twenty years now I've received transmissions from him and a few other other-dimensional voices or beings.

"And the messages have always led to warnings of protecting the planet," she continued. "The human race is instrumental in destroying its own planet. In a time of change, however, we can make a better time. We have the ability to make right that which we have wronged in the past. We are not "bound " by our mistakes. We can choose to turn around and walk away from our past – or we can continue blindly to what is almost certainly our collective doom. We can sing in a higher octave than the end of the world. There's a time of change when we can create with our consciousness a whole new dimension. That is really the only thing that can be done at this point, because so many things are in a desperate way. Both the environment and the political system, governments. We've kind of unraveled our basis for reality, so we need to discover a whole new reality."

Diane Tessman

TESSMAN MEETS TIBUS AS A CHILD

Tessman explained more about Tibus and her relationship with him.

"We describe him as a voice from Earth's future," she began, "but he says he's as real as you or I, if we would look at ourselves and see flesh and blood and three dimensions. Neither Tibus nor I make a big deal out of whether he is a sold, three-dimensional alien, or simply a voice from the future that you might describe as my higher consciousness or future self.

We really don't care how a person considers him. We're really more concerned with getting our message out."

Tessman told the story of how she first met Tibus on her family's farm. She and her family left the farm when Tessman was ten and moved to Florida. Later, as an adult, she lived in the Virgin Islands, Ireland and California, but eventually returned to the same Iowa farm where she is living at present.

"I always dreamed of coming back here," she said, "and a person might wonder why because north Iowa isn't as glamorous as those other places. But I felt a need to come back here and I've been here now for almost five years. I feel that this is where I should be at this time."

As a child, Tessman was playing outside late at night in a backfield behind the barn with her dog. Those were the days, she remarked, when "there were never any security concerns," and a child could play unguarded safely and without fear of harm. She perceived a light coming down from the sky.

"I felt no fear," she said.

Only later, as an adult, did she recall the rest of what happened. While undergoing regressive hypnosis with abduction researcher Dr. R. Leo Sprinkle (for more on Sprinkle, see Chapter Four), Tessman recalled being taken onboard a craft and encountering a man who looked human and had tawny or gold colored hair.

"He was nice looking," she said, "but had an enhanced quality that's hard to put into words. I felt very at ease with him, very safe. He was fatherly. I guess the experience lasted maybe half an hour, forty-five minutes. I feel it was just a preparation, or a reawakening, because I think I was always a soul that was intended to be part of the change times or to ring alarms about the condition of the planet. The encounter was a time to reawaken me, to remind me of a higher purpose.

"And I've never lived, maybe as a result of that," she went on, "a real typical lifetime.

I haven't married, have lived in a lot of places, have always kind of lived in the 'now,' haven't followed tradition. I think that was maybe necessary in order to be available to help other people and to bring my message."

Did Tessman recall any words being spoken to her by Tibus at their first meeting?

"I don't remember words," she answered. "I always stress I don't remember this consciously even now, so it's hard to give additional information. I remember it in hypnosis, and I know hypnosis doesn't have to be the absolute truth, and we really don't present it as such. But if there was a message, maybe given telepathically or just in 'feeling,'—I remember telling Dr. Sprinkle that I cried for joy or happiness or 'belonging' or a happy reminder that I was special. But again, not special in all the world.

"Many people would have had the same feeling," she continued, "regardless of whether they had the same exact experience. The feeling of being loved. And I remember crying during hypnosis, just with the same kind of uncontrolled happiness or the feeling that I was touching home, a true home. There was no verbal message given, but I have always remembered it."

SOME OTHER ENTITIES ARE HEARD FROM

Tessman may not recall any words spoken to her during that first visit with Tibus, but there has certainly been a steady flow of words in the past twenty years, more than enough to make up for that initial silence. Tessman described some of the other entities, other than Tibus, who she also hears from.

"I hear occasionally from somebody who calls himself W'vora the Wizard," she said. "He's somewhat Merlin-like, and perhaps he could be described as an archetypical wizard. Whether he lived or lives eternally as an individual wizard or magical man, I don't know. But he gives messages always connected to Earth. He would be an ancient contact.

"And then I have a future or perhaps I'd say alien contact with a female, a being named Amethysta. A friend came to me and said that in the snows in northern California, they had seen something on the ground and some little beings came out and looked at the snow. This was told to me back in the early 90s. And I feel, and my friend felt correct with it, that this being I started hearing from then named Amethysta was one of the little large-eyed aliens, kind of one of the classic *Close Encounters* aliens, that

90

my friend had first seen in an actual UFO encounter or sighting. Something strange. It was at night, and there was a craft just sitting in the snow, and the beings were looking at the snow or almost playing in it. Maybe taking samples. Anyway, Amethysta comes through fairly often, and she would be alien or certainly 'future.'"

THE PAGAN ENERGIES OF IRELAND

Tessman talked about her interest in UFOs, which included serving stints with both The Mutual UFO Network (MUFON) and the Aerial Phenomenon Research Organization (APRO).

"So my interest was, wow, do these things exist? Are they nuts and bolts? Do people just make up these stories? What part does human psychology play in 'needing' to see them? Sometimes I'm my own biggest skeptic, but over the years, I have not been able to tell myself that there wasn't something to it. And that something is actually an immense phenomenon for the human race."

But when Tessman moved to Ireland in 1989, her interests took a very ancient turn. "I went back to pre-Christian ruins and places in Ireland and got the feeling of it. It's such a magical place. It is almost like nothing has changed over the centuries and that the ancient energies still remain, waiting to be tapped into again. So then I took a swing toward pagan energies, very ancient magic, and what was lost over the years. And while I don't dislike Christianity, I know that so much was taken from pre-Christian times by Christians. Like they put their churches on holy ground and thus kind of covered up the pagan or old ways, the knowledge and the feelings. They took the consort of the goddess, the horned goat consort, and started calling him Satan. That's where that image comes from.

"There were places in Ireland," she continued, "where there were rags tied on trees. They were prayer trees. It was a sacred tree where they would say a prayer and then tie a rag on. The poor tree, I think it probably died after a while because it was just covered with rags. That was a pagan practice, but now of course it's all Catholic Christians. I became aware of how much our ancient ancestors gave us, and how it's been totally lost since Christianity came in and completely took over. Many holy men and women were put to death because in pre-Christian times women were every bit as important if not more so than the men. There was open worship of the goddess back then."

THE PROCESS TESSMAN USES

Tessman said that as the year 2000 came around, she meshed both her UFO and pagan backgrounds and has since heard from everyone from Nikola Tesla to Gaia, or the living spirit of Mother Earth, the Earth herself.

"I've been told that I'm one of the few who manages to bring in all the past, the future, UFOs, ecology, occasional comments on politics, Earth changes, upheavals, increasing volcano activity. We just kind of covered the spectrum," she said, "without claiming to be absolute authorities on any of it. But for about twenty years we've been talking about the change times and what would come with the year 2000. We had mentioned transportation catastrophes and odd things, huge things happening. We didn't predict September 11 per se, but for twenty years we've kind of been saying things were coming unraveled anyway.

"I guess we're more generally concerned," she went on, "with the responsibility of mankind. It isn't a popular thing to say because I've found that humans always want Tibus to tell them exactly, to give them a set of rules, and that isn't what we're about. A lot of what we've said has been good guidance. I don't pretend to be Jean Dixon and putting my thumb right on things.

"We just feel it's so foolish for the human race to be destroying the planet that gave it life, that it stands on. We feel global warming is worse than is reported, and we're diverted with so many things that matter to a few people—everything from OJ Simpson to Jon Benet. I mean, they're tragic things, but they're not earthshaking. And yet we can see a volcano or an earthquake that takes a few thousand lives and we barely hear about it because it's in the Third World or across the globe and we don't connect to those people. And we really must."

Just how does Tessman receive these transmissions? I asked her if she simply heard a voice speaking.

"No, I don't," she said. "I'm kind of glad I don't actually. I can best describe it as a shared consciousness. People have come great distances to have a channeling. If I'm channeling in person, I would prefer to close my eyes and simply concentrate. It's not showy. My favorite way of channeling is writing or typing. My fingers just fly. The concepts come to me in completed form, at least a paragraph's worth, and then I have to catch it and write it down correctly. Tibus would rework it if I didn't write it down right the first time. But they just come to me in completed thoughts.

"Now, again, that isn't showy, so whether it's Diane having semi-brilliant input or thoughts, could be, but it seems to me it's something more. And it seems to people who stay with me a while, and there have been hundreds if not thousands over the years, that it's something more. It's a heightened form of concentration, and I feel a shared consciousness, that there's another consciousness that becomes overlaid with mine, which is very similar to mine, perhaps in metaphysical terms a twin flame, but certainly compatible but with more perspective. Like it's flying higher over the planet than I ever could and looking in time and space, the future and the past."

TIBUS SPEAKS

At this point in the interview, Diane began to read to me from one of Tibus' more recent messages, received in February of 2002. Any number of events will have happened in the meantime before this book is in the hands of readers, but much of what Tibus had to say would be relevant in any time.

"Hello, my friends, in this perilous time on Earth," Tibus begins. "Each month the situation grows more critical. This is the time to find your divine power within as never before. If you will but perceive you will feel our presence within you. If you but perceive, you will see us. If you will but be, you will be with us. Sadly, the human race is in the process of fragmenting itself as never before. It points a finger at self and proclaims itself an infidel. It points a finger at self and proclaims itself an Evil Axis. This is a death spiral, but those of enlightened consciousness need not go down with the ship. This is the brilliant and beautiful silver lining to the dark cloud, a fresh new start, a brand new day, a beautiful dawn.

"Is the New World Order somehow behind recent events so as to institute military rule? Or are Mid-Eastern terrorists alone to blame? In reality, it makes little difference if you realize the human race is one. One consciousness with one voice. This can be a voice of love, but all too often it is the voice of hatred.

"The sad fact is that a few super-wealthy individuals in huge global corporations have stolen shamelessly from the common people the world over. Worst of all, they have stolen the resources and now the life-force of the planet herself. However, we do not condone those who practice violence because this only increases the downward spiral. They play the same game with the same rules as the powers that be. The two will cancel each other out and fade into oblivion, which is the darkness of the past.

"You have only to hold on, to sing your song, and to keep your eye on the highest star. We would like to give you a new meditation, a magical stream of though in these days, which we know are extremely difficult for you. These are not just words. They hold great power. And the special words are" Be healed. Be whole. Be divine. Trees, branching, reaching to the sky. Be healed. Animals, life-forms, celebrating life. Be whole. Bird soaring joyfully toward heaven. Be divine. Oceans rising and ebbing, living sea. Be healed. Humankind, manifesting higher consciousness from within. Be whole. Gaia, living spirit of the Earth Mother. Be healed. Be whole. Be divine.

"My friends, you can use different subjects of concern as well as trees, animals and oceans, which we just gave you. You can put in specific concerns, such as the redwoods, which are starting to show disease, similar to the Western oak. Or the koala, which was so hurt by the fires in Australia. The descriptive concepts, such as the branches reaching to the skies, may express whatever you wish as you concentrate on new subjects.

"However, the miraculous words: Be healed, be whole, be divine, should remain the same. There are several crucial forks in the road at this point in the change times, and our cleansing/healing days are very important."

HOW IT'S ALL SUPPOSED TO WORK

Tessman explained that the "cleansing/healing days" are listed in her monthly newsletter and are designed to focus the energy of her readers on healing the planet on specific calendar days. A kind of group meditation takes place that attempts to deal with certain environmental and political problems from a distance.

"The whales, for instance," Tessman said, "are suffering greatly with the Navy's ultra-low frequency sonar program. It makes the whales' inner ears bleed, then they beach themselves. So we're trying to influence that. They're still doing their experiments, but we work on specific subjects like that each month."

The point, of course, is that simply meditating as a group on specific problems can somehow improve the situation. Tessman made reference to psychiatrist Carl Gustav Jung and stated her heartfelt belief in a mass human consciousness.

"There is a wolf hum that makes a wolf act like a wolf," she explained, "and a cat hum and so forth. There's a human hum. I don't think we realize how dynamic and powerful that can be and that we can change it. There are examples in history where it changed so quickly. The Renaissance I think was one of those, coming from out of the dark ages.

"The 60s," she continued. "Of course, I'm a child of the 60s, and if it hadn't gotten bogged down in too many drugs and political violence, kind of taking on the establishment when there wasn't a chance of winning anyway—and violence is wrong—but there was a change overnight that did have some evolutionary and spiritual good things there, but it didn't quite make it.

"And then September 11 is an example of, just in an instant, complete change. We said recently that we understand, this is from Tibus more than me, we understand the patriotism and how people feel threatened by what happened, and humiliated. It was a terrible thing that happened. But it's taken the country down to a more narrow viewpoint, that we embrace only other Americans. We don't have as much empathy as perhaps we did before September 11 for others. In a way, it was a setback spiritually, but we're sure there will be a silver lining to that cloud.

"Everything always works for the better eventually. We truly feel that we have the power in our hands to raise the frequency. And this means a whole new reality, something people would hardly realize had happened. It doesn't take that many to reach enlightenment. You don't need everybody to awaken to what we're doing to the planet and really get in contact.

"I think another aspect of it," Tessman continued, "is the need to really get in contact with the female side of the creator spirit. Certainly in Islam and Christianity, the male has ruled for years, and he's there, too. The   creator spirit is part male, but any creation takes a male and a female. That's universal. And the female creator spirit has been put down to witches and goblins for so many years. But a part of the awakening needs to happen with what I feel is a critical mass of humans. I don't know how many. I don't think it's 144,000 or two or ten million. I don't know a number, but I think that the actual hum, the human hum, which makes us what we are, can affect everybody on the planet from just a certain number reaching enlightenment."

According to Tessman, the "consciousness frequency" she just described must undergo palpable, real-world changes for mankind to survive.

"I don't think we'll ever get out of certain predicaments with the frequency of the consciousness that we're currently on," she cautioned. "We keep falling into wars. We keep fragmenting ourselves. We hate the Russians and we hate the Afghans. That's not looking at ourselves as one person, but in fact, when they bleed, we bleed. We are one.

95

We have the same emotions. We don't want our family to be hurt. We're the same. But nobody sees that."

WHAT THE NEW AGE WILL BE LIKE

My next question to Tessman was, given that she and others finally do succeed in raising our collective hum, what will the results be like? How will our lives be different?

Her answer sounded more pragmatic and level-headed than I expected.

"I don't see it as going to heaven," she replied, "or as a paradise. At least I hope it's not because I think that might be boring. I see it as an enhanced and new reality. Part of trying to visualize that new reality involves the question of what will happen to those who don't feel the same way. Well, I'm not pointing a finger or condemning them to anything. I don't have all the answers. I suspect that since it's a human hum, it would sweep most people along. And I suppose somebody who can't adapt in terms of evolution would kind of fade into oblivion or into the past. But I can't in solid terms exactly say because I'm not the one setting it up. I'm just so sure that there can be a revolutionary upgrade in the hum.

"But again, it's certainly not a vision of heaven," she said. "Maybe I should say it would be an enhanced Earth, one that was brighter and cleaner and more peaceful. As far as the damage that's been done to Earth—the global warming, the ozone, the oceans, contaminations, the coral reefs are dying. There are things dying right and left. There are entire species being wiped out and nobody really bats an eye. I think, since we control reality, that many of those lost species could exist in a new Earth, almost miraculously coming back. We're certainly capable of it technically.

"So I see an enhanced Earth," she said, "a higher octave, but not yet a high C. Just a better reality that would sweep across the land rather magically and overnight. I pointed out that evolution doesn't always take millions and billions of years, as we're taught in school. There are a lot of examples of changes happening nearly overnight with certain species. It does work that way sometimes."

Just what kind of changes may be in store for our species, good old humankind?

"I think that we'll be able to perceive much more," Tessman said, "in a way that you almost can't put into words, a whole other dimension. We'll have knowledge of the whole self, which could include other lifetimes, or at least glimpses into other

96

experiences we've had as souls or consciousnesses. We think with our right or left brain, and I've also felt that a way of expressing that change is perhaps by saying that there is a bridge in the brain that isn't really activated in most people. It's in the third eye area, but it would be a conduit between the right and left brain, and could perhaps be activated through spiritual evolution. Or maybe we would use more than ten percent of our giant brains, which would be good, too.

"But it's a little more than just the brain. It's also the soul. Maybe we'd use more than ten percent of our souls. But you can word it so many ways."

PLEAS AND WARNINGS FROM MOTHER EARTH

When I asked Tessman if she had any final comments, she answered by reading another transmission from one of her other-dimensional friends. This time, the voice of Gaia, or Mother Earth, presented mankind with some rather interesting pleas and warnings. Tessman said she had received this transmission on January 17, 2002.

"Of all the times you have spoken of me," Gaia began, "you have not heard directly from me. And yet many times you have. My volcanoes, my mountains, my rivers, my oceans, all are me. All are my children. They have their own persona, but they are me. You have heard messages from Mother Mary. She is me, and I am her. And yet we are two different awarenesses experiencing different experiences. Hers was the human path, the religious path, and finally she grew to be bigger than these. She is part of the cosmos, part of the All, part of the One. Mine was the path of nature, for I am nature. But I grew, and I am part of the cosmos, the All, the One.

"Mary and Gaia, we are twins in the mirror of reality. My spirit is strong. I am as strong as I am because the few like you have connected to me, reflected me, given me strength and healing. My physical body is troubled. This trouble grows, mushrooming, snowballing. Problems cause new problems. I will not stoop to list what has happened and who is to blame. You, my enlightened friend, are not among those to blame. No, you have helped. Not all humans are bad. Not all humans were a mistake.

"I am a vibrant, breathing ball of life. I will be cleansed. I will be healed. I am too strong to die. Other balls out there in space did not have my luck. Most could not sustain sacred life at the level I do. A very high level of life, a great diversity of life, is mine. I am very proud. Some living worlds have been zapped by asteroids or gamma rays or what have you. Life stops abruptly. All life stops. I have been spared. My location in the galaxy is fortunate. The spring is coming, when I do my magic as only I can.

"Join me then as you have never joined me before. Our spirits will entwine. You will heal me. I will heal you.

"If you fear that you have become an Earth worshiper, know that I am the creator personified within the planet's atmosphere. Your belief in God is intact. And if you are a proud Earth worshiper in the first place, I thank you for perceiving the creator spirit so keenly. The truth is that if you do not stand on me, you do not stand. If you do not breathe my air, you do not breathe. Why are angels so high and the Earth beneath your feet so lowly? Go stand on an angel and breathe angel air then.

"But I promised I would not show anger, an anger which masks the pain I am in. I do not want to be worshiped above all others. I merely want to be treasured for what I am. The only world you truly know, the world on which you were born, the world on which you will die, the world on which you will transcend to a new life, the world which gave you and a million other life-forms life. I have many layers of dimensions and there are other worlds out there. They are my brothers and my sisters. Many of you have known and will know life on them and in other realities as well.

"I do not mean to be demanding, but you must let it be known that I am in pain. I am hurt and wounded. I need you to be my child with no conditions, for you are my child. I need you to reflect me and pay homage to my magic gift of life. I need you to know that when you recognize that you are not going against your religion, you are only expanding its vistas. I need you to heal me. I need you to guide my anger. I need you to help me transcend so you can transcend. I am strong. We will go on. I am Gaia."

Finally, Tessman said, "So I guess that's a good place to conclude it. That's really my main message as it's evolved over the years. It all kind of comes to that, I think."

If you are interested in learning more about Diane Tessman and her channeling, write to her at: **P.O. Box 352, Saint Ansgar, IA, 50472** to receive a free sample copy of her monthly newsletter.

Chapter Ten
Judith Bluestone Polich: Ancient Prophecies For A New World

"They called that time preceding a world age shift 'pachacuti.' Now, 'pacha' means all of the physical manifestations, and 'cuti' means to turn upside down. So a really tumultuous time, a time of overturning of time/space reality, always preceded a world shift. Sometimes that could take the form of catastrophic physical events in which the threads to the past were broken and so a new understanding of reality emerged. Other times it might be more of a psychic event, something that happened at a deeper structural level, that caused reality to shift. So certainly we're in a time a time of pachacuti now, a time of very rapid change, a change of our understanding of reality."

Judith Bluestone Polich is the author of ***Return of the Children of Light: Incan and Mayan Prophecies For a New World*** (Bear and Company, 2001). Polich's book is an intelligently written examination of prophecies many hundreds of years old that seem to be extremely relevant to our present era. The book is also an earnest record of her personal spiritual journey into the still very much alive mystical energies of that period so long ago. Polich earned her law degree in 1981. Since then, she has worked as a transactional attorney, dealing mainly in wills, trusts and estates, real estate, business law and contracts. Given the disciplined, pragmatic temperament required to practice law, it is perhaps surprising to realize that Polich is also deeply immersed in the ancient world of Incan and Mayan prophecy and the promises they make of a new form of mankind and the changed world in which we will dwell.

In Polich's mind, however, both parts of herself are in a pleasant harmony with one another.

"I can be someone who has mystical experiences and a lawyer," Polich said, "and there's no contradiction. We can be more multi-dimensional, if you will, in that sense."

THE MYSTICAL EXPERIENCES THAT STARTED IT ALL

The long and winding road that led to Polich's ***Return of the Children of Light*** began with a mystical experience she had twenty years earlier. Shortly after leaving both her home and her marriage behind in Madison, Wisconsin, and bound for Boston to start a new life, she found herself magnetically drawn to a peak called Mount Blue in the state of Maine. Without quite understanding why, she grabbed a blanket and

Judith Bluestone Polich

ascended the mountain, where she found herself quite alone and began to meditate.

"Suddenly," she writes, "as the sun rose, my entire being was flooded—first with wave after wave of brilliant white light, then with wave after wave of iridescent rainbow light. It filled me with deep love, a sense of well-being, and a penetrating clarity."

In a later interview with me, Polich looked back at the experience with genuine awe.

"I had no idea, really, what it was," she said. "I didn't know if it was a charka opening or what was going on at that time, but I think it was probably the first real mystical experience that I've had. I don't even know what I would have called it at that time. But it was so luminous. And at that time I would not have connected it to any other mythologies. It was years before I began to do any study or work on any of the sites in the Americas and to make a connection, as strong a connection between any type of mystical experience and ancient sites. For a long time I tended to discount these things, as many people do, or just forget about them because they don't fit into the reality that I'm normally in."

Return of the Children of Light also includes another mystical experience that had a great deal of influence on Polich. On her first trip to Teotihuacan, located near Mexico City, she ascended to the top of the Pyramid of the Sun, one of numerous ancient ruins she would visit over the years. She was accompanied by her teacher and friend, a shaman named don Miguel Ruiz, who began to perform some kind of ritual with another young shaman, or in the native tongue, a "nagual."

"I had no idea what they were doing," Polich writes. "Then I saw to my astonishment that their hands were made of millions of stars, swirling galaxies of light, the very matrix of the universe. I quickly looked away in disbelief, thinking that what I had seen could not possibly be true. Yet when I looked back, I saw the same vision."

In our interview, Polich had this to say: "That was something that happened with my eyes wide open. It wasn't a dream. It wasn't just a meditation. It wasn't anything I saw in my mind's eye. It was something I saw with my physical eye. A lot of people have inward experiences, where they'll have a visualization or something like that. This was with the five senses, which put it in a different category. Because it was easy for me to discount something that happened in a dream state, or to discount something that was an image in my third eye or something. But it was very hard for me to discount this.

"Our linear mind is so powerful," she continued, "and that part of our mind which is the part that most people are familiar with is really designed for categorizing. So it will put it in a category and say, 'Oh, okay, unusual experience.' In a way, you have to step outside those boundaries and allow in another way of perceiving to really validate those kinds of experiences."

LOCATION, LOCATION, LOCATION

When Polich writes about many of her experiences in far away places—like Peru and Mexico and Central America—the geographical location often seems to be central to the nearly supernatural energies she experiences there. Like they say in the real estate business Polich works in as an attorney, it all comes down to location, location, location.

I asked her if she believed that the ancient sites she visited really do have spiritual powers of their own that are rooted in a particular place.

"I do," she said. "And that is really based on personal experience, my own and other people's, and to some degree things that others have written about—people who have studied ancient sites and the subjective reports of people who have visited the sites and recounted their experiences. It's not like there's any objective data. It's all subjective data.

"I feel they're special places," she explained, "and that they may hold special energies. If you just think of them as being a special energy field—you can enter into a cathedral and you'll feel a special energy field. In some ways, that can come into being just because of the number of people who've gone there over the years and centuries and held that kind of energy. Most of the great cathedrals in England are built upon much older sites. We know that. So there's a long history of engagement that has occurred there."

It was after her first visits to spiritually powerful sites in Peru and Machu Picchu in 1997 that something jelled for Polich and she began to write her book.

"I came back and I just couldn't stop writing," she said, "until I had a manuscript. It was almost as if there was some kind of blueprint that came through at that point, but I had to flesh it all out. I was drawn to a lot of different resources to do that. I was quite clear that I wasn't going to write a book that was just anecdotal. It came out of my attempt to pull together and make sense out of things, because I guess I'd seen a whole coalescing. And I'd read enough from different sources that the threads started to make a weaving basically."

THE INCAN PROPHECIES

Polich next talked about her initial discovery of the Incan prophecies that seem to have such bearing on the present world.

The prophecies came to her attention by way of anthropologist Juan Nunez del Prado, who "has been sort of a bridge person between the indigenous people and the ancient teachings of Peru and everybody else," she said.

"Juan's father, Oscar Nunez del Prado, who was also an anthropologist, 'rediscovered,' if you will, the Q'ero people who lived in the very high elevations of Peru and who had very little contact with the outside world until about fifty years ago."

Polich explained that because of their isolation, the Q'ero's native teachings had remained a little more intact than was the case with other indigenous peoples.

"They hadn't quite fallen under the grip," she said, "of the conquest by the Spanish and then of course by the Catholic Church.

"And among their teachings were prophecies," she continued. "The prophecies are somewhat energy based, because these people have an ability to perceive reality more energetically than the rest of us. So their prophecies talk about consciousness being divided into seven levels. They believe that most humans are presently at the second and third levels of consciousness. Their prophecies talk about a coming time in which there will be a leap into a fifth level of consciousness and that this new consciousness is a much more holistic, much more energetically-based consciousness—very different than our way of perceiving the world now."

All of the Incan prophecies, Polich explained, relate to different cycles of time and different world ages.

"We, in the Western mindset, tend to perceive things in a linear manner, but many indigenous people and their calendars are much more cyclic in terms of their understanding of time."

THE MAYAN CALENDAR AND THE YEAR 2012

Talk shifted from the Incas to the subtleties of the Mayan calendar.

"The classical Maya were really much earlier in time," Polich began, "and they of course have a very elaborate calendar system. Their understanding of world ages isn't based on shifts in energy, on shifts in perception, and shifts in understanding of time/space, say, like the Inca. But the Mayan calendar is very precisely based. It's based on a concept from astronomy called 'precession.' The idea being that the ancient Maya were able to track these very long cycles of time, including the 25,800 year cycle of time that is the 'precessional cycle.' Their prophecies really come from an understanding of that precessional cycle, and an understanding that at four times during that cycle the solstice or the equinox sun would come into direct alignment with the center of our galaxy."

And after waiting for thousands of years for that alignment, what is our reward?

"That alignment, that union," she explained, "which would be for them the force of the divine masculine and the divine feminine, would somehow bring a shift in human consciousness. You can look at it as a rebalancing of the human psyche that would lead to a time of spiritual rebirth and renewal—a similar kind of time that the Andeans predict in terms of the shift to the fifth level of consciousness. Both of those time periods from both cultures correlate with the year 2012, which the mythologies of course of dozens of ancient cultures do as well. It's been predicted for a long time as a big shift in awareness.

"The 2012 date, from the Mayan point of view," she continued, "marks the end of their current world age and the end of a full precessional cycle and the beginning of another. From Inca, Aztec and Toltec tradition, they would say we're entering now into the period of the sixth sun, again because they have a slightly different way of measuring time. There are actually about twenty different calendar systems that are still in use in the Americas."

The Western way of measuring time, by contrast, is linear.

"The perspective in all the Judeo-Christian traditions," she said, "is that all of their calendar systems view time in a linear way. They didn't view it cyclically. So if you view things in a linear way, you have a clear beginning, a clear Creation, and you have an end. I think that's why those systems are a lot more apocalyptic, because they're based on linear calendars."

THE INCA AND A TIME OF RAPID CHANGE

I next asked Polich if the prophecies she had written about had anything similar to the "Earth Changes" so commonly believed to precede the coming golden New Age.

"Well, sure," she replied, "the concept in Inca tradition was that there would be a

104

series of events that would precede a world age shift. They called their world ages 'suns,' a time when they would enter a new sun. It was almost as if they believed that the light coming into our solar system from the broader universe somehow was triggering a change, a shift in perception, a shift in the understanding of space/time.

"They called that time preceding a world age shift 'pachacuti.' Now, 'pacha' means all of the physical manifestations, and 'cuti' means to turn upside down. So a really tumultuous time, a time of overturning of time/space reality, always preceded a world shift. Sometimes that could take the form of catastrophic physical events in which the threads to the past were broken and so a new understanding of reality emerged. Other times it might be more of a psychic event, something that happened at a deeper structural level, that caused reality to shift. So certainly we're in a time a time of pachacuti now, a time of very rapid change, a change of our understanding of reality.

"And there are a lot of ways to look at that," she went on. "You can say, 'Oh, the world's going to implode,' or whatever. And it may be that the pace of change is moving really quickly. Obviously the world we live in now is very, very different than the world people lived in a hundred years ago. If somebody were to pop on Earth having been asleep for a hundred years, they definitely would feel out of place and know that there's been a total shift in reality and our understanding of space/time in the last hundred years, as indeed there has been.

"So it doesn't always have to be earthquakes and major floods," she said, "but certainly in prehistory we know those kinds of things happened also. But I really don't find these prophecies as particularly apocalyptic in the sense that I would attach to Judeo-Christian and other more fundamentalist ways of looking at things."

SIGNS OF HOPE

In ways similar to what New Age channeler Diane Tessman had to say, Polich believes we have a rise in the frequency of human consciousness to look forward to.

"From the perspective of the Andean teachings," Polich said, "where everything is energy or frequency based, that's really what they're talking about. They're saying the problem is that most humans are now operating at a very low level frequency of consciousness. They're operating at what they call the second and third levels of consciousness, but there is an emergence of a new consciousness that is probably what they would call the fourth level of consciousness, one that's more holistic. It can even contemplate the idea of an energy shift. But they say really when we hit the fifth level that that's when the Golden Age emerges."

Again, that may not be as easy as it sounds.

"There's always some pain," Polich said, "in letting go of a viewpoint, a philosophy, whatever it is we're attached to that no longer serves us. But, for example, part of what the Mayan prophecies are telling us is that this wonderful alignment in the sky between the solstice sun, the masculine principle, and the very center of the galaxy, the feminine principle, that these polarities have to come back into balance and into a new balance, a new harmony. In other words, the patriarchy is coming to an end. Obviously that's going to be very painful to some people who are very vested in one way of viewing things.

"I really think that it's hard work to change," she continued, "and whatever the new consciousness is, it is coming through us. It's not coming through anybody else. It's not going to be imposed on us from the outside, from some magical wand of God. The point is that the collective humanity is evolving. How does evolution proceed? It isn't always slow and incremental. Sometimes evolutionary change can happen really quickly."

THE POSSIBILITY OF A UFO FACTOR

I next raised the possibility of UFOs and their alien occupants somehow being part of the overall mix.

"One premise of my book," Polich responded, "is that, if you really look back at the mythic record, there's evidence of contact on this planet with other beings that has been happening for a long, long period of time. I tend to believe that, and I also tend to believe that if everything is really energy, and if we have contact with a different energy, or a different frequency energy, we're going to perceive it in a way that's familiar to our brain and the way we have adapted in our environment. So if I'm looking at a UFO, and I'm really looking for little green men, then that's what I'll see. If someone else is coming from a different perspective and a different way of having learned to conceptualize things in their brain, then they're going to see something else. But neither of these differences in perception negate the fact that we're dealing with some kind of 'other energy' phenomenon."

At another point in the interview, Polich was talking about Incan prophecies regarding Wiraccocha, the Creator-God of Incan mythology.

"The way Juan Nunez del Prado explained Wiraccocha to me," she said, "is that Wiraccocha is the force that comes periodically and brings the new order. Reorders reality in a way."

I couldn't resist asking if the coming of Wiraccocha as a supernatural entity with the power to literally change reality might be an ancient reference to some kind of alien.

Polich considered for a moment, then replied, "Well, you know, if you travel around in Peru and parts of Central America, there's certainly a lot of indication that there's a residue of mythology, of belief that these were star-seeded cultures, that their ancestors came from the stars, that Wiraccocha wasn't from this world—those kinds of things."

THE DIVINE MASCULINE AND FEMININE

So where are we now? What is the current state of affairs in this sea of pachacuti, of the world order turning upside down, that we now find ourselves in so uncomfortably?

"A lot of contemporary writers and thinkers," Polich said, "are saying that we're coming to a time of rebalancing of the human psyche, a rebalancing of the masculine and feminine, a time of sacred marriage and a birth of a new consciousness that is much more matrix-based, that is much more part of a collective wholeness. We're really birthing in a way a new mythology. I don't think of mythology as old and dead. I think of it as the vibrant system of beliefs that shape our reality.

"A big part of this birth of a new consciousness, of new belief systems, of breaking free of old belief systems, does have to do with a rebalancing that the Mayan prophecies talk about, of the rebalancing of the masculine and feminine within the external world as well as within the human psyche. So I think these are multi-tiered prophecies. They work at a lot of different levels. And I think that's part of why I find them so rich and exciting.

"I don't think we always realize," she continued, "the degree to which we are directed by those concepts, or what you would call archetypes. You know Carl Jung and Frank Waters both predicted some time ago that there would be a coming time with this shift into a New Age or a New Consciousness and what that would be about was a rebalancing of the human psyche, as the dominant ego-based part of ourselves becomes less dominant and the suppressed feminine comes more into balance. I think that we see that all over the world, and in our lives, but it's an inside job. In order for the shift in consciousness to happen, it's an internal event that has to be expressed externally."

Meanwhile, the lessons from history are painfully obvious.

"All of these ancient civilizations," Polich explained, "like the Inca and the Maya, Egypt and Sumeria, many of our great civilizations believed that creation resulted from a union between the divine masculine and the divine feminine. In the last 6,000 years or so, we've forgotten about that. The evolving belief systems that became dominant gave us the religious systems we have now. They're all patriarchally based. Those are very different 'belief in creation' systems than those of ancient peoples.

"But I think we're at a time now where we're finding that these old belief systems just don't work so well. Look at the idea of quantum physics. When the implications of quantum physics are really felt and understood, you have to start thinking about reality very differently.

"The idea of rebalancing," Polich concluded, "where that part of our self and our psyche that's been suppressed, the feminine, can now re-emerge and come into a new balance, maybe means that we can all be more psychic, we can all have a more developed mystical side."

PALESTINIAN POLICE INVESTIGATE ALIEN KIDNAPPING ATTEMPT

On October 19,1997 the Israeli newsmagazine Yerushalayim reported that the Palestinian Police were investigating their first alien kidnapping.

The event occurred three days before when a young girl, Suha A'anam from the village of Dir Al Awasan near Tulkarem, was rescued by fellow villagers from the clutches of an alien. The Police report states that Suha, a grade ten pupil, was standing on her 2nd floor balcony when suddenly an alien began pulling her left hand. She screamed hysterically, alerting neighbours to the scene just in time to save her. She was taken to Tulkarem Hospital with scratches to her arm.

A neighbour told the Police that she heard a noise like a helicopter, looked out her window and saw "a whirlpool in the air, spreading ash everywhere" opposite Suha's balcony.

Two other witnesses saw aliens the same week. Six days before, sixteen year old Muhand Faras was walking home from school when he came upon a strange being of a man's size but with a small "root" in the middle of its face. It's skin was colored "like a frog's," it had two tiny hands with three fingers on each and long fingernails. The alien made a threatening, clawing gesture at Muhand's face, screamed something and "flew to the sky." He does not know where the creature flew because he "was too frightened to look at it anymore and thought it might shoot something dangerous" at him.

Three days later, an engineer, Raid A'anam saw a black creature in the sky just before sundown. He told police investigators that the outline of the flying object was "human with two arms and two legs."

Palestinian Police have since set up ambushes to trap the "intruders" and put an end to the villagers' terror. Needless to say, many villagers believe the Israeli intelligence agency, the Shabak is behind the sightings. When asked why the Israelis would stage such an incident, the villagers answered, "To scare us."

Chapter Eleven
The Astrological Forecasts Of Dr. Louis Turi

"The age of ignorance and of religion being classified as going to a church or synagogue is dying, and it's being replaced by the new Age of Aquarius. Mankind has to wake up and free its spirit and realize again that the true church is the universe and that the true twelve apostles are a reflection of the twelve signs of the zodiac. And that is the ultimate religion that will bless the world and will bring the option for peace and harmony."

Dr. Louis Turi can be said to have a certain advantage when it comes to being a prophet and an astrologist. He was born in Provence, France, the same town as Nostradamus himself. But Turi came to the subjects of prophecy and astrology only after he first made a career for himself as a musician, graduating from the Royal School of Music in London in 1976.

He moved to the United States soon after in hopes of promoting his musical career here. A few years later, however, he was forced to find other ways of supporting himself and took up the business of astrology full-time. Turi received a metaphysical doctorate from the Light Institute in Sacramento, California, and began to develop his own form of astrology, which he calls "Astropsychology."

Since then, he has been a successful lecturer, teacher and writer and has given practical and spiritual guidance to thousands of clients worldwide as well as having appeared numerous times on radio and television.

TURI'S UFO ENCOUNTERS

Turi was prodded into the study of astrology by a series of encounters with UFOs that began in his childhood.

"As long as I live," Turi wrote in an account of what happened to him at age seven, "I shall never forget that particular moment. That unworldly episode would haunt me the rest of my life. Surprised and horrified, I watched four strange creatures. They were about four feet tall. These eerie 'visitors' were staring at me from the bottom of my bed.

They were cautiously looking at me with their enlarged piercing black eyes. It was as if they were wondering how I could see them. I was in shock and unable to bring forward a single sound. My throat was tightened as if in a knot, and even if I wanted, not a sound would come out of my mouth.

Dr. Louis Turi

"I swiftly brought the blanket above my head and hid away in the bed," he continued. "In spite of the cutting cold, I was perspiring and wondering why those little 'monkeys' were here. I was desperately waiting for those 'visitors' to go away. Finally, after what seemed to be an eternity, I slowly pulled the blanket away from my eyes and peered out into the semidarkness. To my extreme surprise, one of them seemingly anticipated my move. He was right there, less than an inch from my petrified face. It was too much for me that night and I simply passed out."

Turi would also encounter UFOs and their alien occupants as an adolescent and a fully-grown adult. His most recent experience took place on August 11, 1991, while traveling with his wife Bridget on the freeway to Los Angeles.

"We were supposed to be twenty minutes away from home," he recounted, "but we ended up past the city of Los Angeles. We had been literally transported in time and space."

Later, under hypnotic regression, Turi learned what had happened during that "missing time."

"Me, Bridget and the car," he explained, "were sucked into the belly of a flying saucer. I felt like something had to be done, so to speak, but I didn't know what it was. So I went back home and I started to literally paint my entire house with astrological symbols and UFOs and all this weird stuff."

NOSTRADAMUS AND ASTROLOGY IN EARNEST

Turi began to dig deeply into the study of astrology as never before.

"I began to put my hand on anything I could put my hand on," he said, "and swallow it and digest it, but it never really made any sense to me. After digging into this type of modern astrology, I was going nowhere. So I went back home, to the Nostradamus museum, and his house, and I started to dig into his work in a way that I never did before.

"I realized that Nostradamus," he continued, "didn't have a watch, he didn't have a computer, he didn't have calendars as we have today. Meantime, he's the most fantastic and accurate astrologer/prophet of all time. So I just used common sense, and I decided to eliminate all the mathematical jargon of modern astrology, and I started to display it in a much more open, simplistic, cleaner way."

"And then I realized," he went on, "how incredibly accurate this method was, and how simple to assimilate, to the point where I started to make all kinds of predictions. So that's basically how it all started."

Turi's new streamlined astrological method emphasized symbolism as opposed to mere numbers.

"You go and listen to any astrologer nowadays," he said, "and they're not astrologers—they're astronomers. They use mathematics, they use numbers, and that confuses the perception of the symbolism, which is the essence of the stars. It is to me so much common sense to use intuition and symbolism, because you don't go into the universal mind with a microscope."

Along with eschewing the mathematics of astrology, Turi also makes no attempt to decipher the prophecies of Nostradamus either.

"In order for anybody to use the Nostradamus' quatrains," he began, "one has to have all the tools that are needed. Meaning of course, speaking our local dialect, called the Provencal, and speaking probably Italian, Greek, etc. You also have to practice his type of astrology. And again, he didn't have a watch or a computer or any kind of machine. He was using a very, very unique system.

"So when somebody out there says that, 'Oh, May 9 California is going to go under the ocean, because famous blah, blah, blah said so,' and then May 9 comes and nothing happens, who is to blame? The writer who was trying to make a few bucks on the name of Nostradamus and hurting his integrity, or Nostradamus? This is why I always back off in terms of using his quatrains, because even though I have all the tools, I was born there, I practiced astrology, I still would not go there because I don't want to hurt his integrity just to try and make a name for myself. I don't want to put his name in jeopardy. This guy is special, very special.

"I am using his technique," Turi continued, "and I have my own feelings, astrologically speaking, of what's ahead of us. Part of astrology is very, very rational. It's also an art, which means a blend of intuition and high science, coming from the celestial bodies interacting with the Earth. We are all under the jurisdiction of the stars, of course. And I have the ability to perceive that and see it unfolding in the future."

THE HEAD AND TAIL OF THE DRAGON

The discussion began to move toward some of Turi's own predictions, but there was still some more groundwork to lay first. Turi explained his personal method of

112

astrological prediction in more detail.

"All my predictions," he said, "are based upon the dragon's head and the dragon's tail. This is what Nostradamus uses in many ways. That's the most powerful change imposed on the world. It is imposed by the dragon, which moves, every two years, backwards within the celestial nature of things. It is not exactly a planet. It's more of a spiritual thing that's very difficult for scientists to rationalize. You have to have full knowledge of the working of the universal mind, and you've got to combine this with a very powerful intuition to understand how the dragon works.

"The dragon is a spiritual energy," he continued. "This is why modern astrology doesn't even deal with it, because they cannot touch it and science needs to be able to touch it. But the impact is more obvious than anything else in your chart. It's very difficult to pinpoint the dragon because it's like a negative energy."

DR. TURI'S DARKEST PREDICTION

In any case, however the head and tail of the dragon are ultimately understood, Turi was ready to make a prediction of his own.

"The tail of the dragon," he said, "will be entering Scorpio on April the 14th, 2003. And it will stay in this very devastating, killing, deadly sign until—it's going to go retrograde of course—until December 26, which will be a Sunday, of 2004. Now, because America was born in July, a Cancer, if you count five from July you will end up in November, which affects the fifth house of the chart of the United States. And the fifth house is the house of children. So with the tail of the dragon in the fifth house of children, you can have a hell of a lot of body bags ready because a lot of kids are going to lose their lives. That's my prediction.

"The tail of the dragon will be there for about a year and a half to two years," he continued. "It indicates that a serious, absolutely incredible drama of death will be suffered by children."

The unhappy alignment of Scorpio has already produced what Turi calls "this killer generation. Scorpio is the sign of death, and this generation shoots themselves in our high schools and universities."

Obviously, we can only wait until the appointed time to see if Turi is correct. Having suffered the shock and torment of 9/11, it seems to many people that anything is possible now.

Turi also discussed predictions he made days after the 9/11 attacks.

"I mentioned that Osama bin Laden and Saddam Hussein are friends," he said. "They are very good friends, from day one. And of course President Bush did not finish the job when he [went to war with Iraq in 1991], because Saddam Hussein had the head of the dragon in Sagittarius by birth, so he is very well protected against foreigners. That's why this country went to his doorstep but we didn't kill him, because the head of the dragon protected him. But the tail of the dragon is on him now, so that's changed. Everything has changed. He's not going to be lucky anymore."

Turi said that, in a lecture he delivered days after the attack, he was the first to make the connection between bin Laden and Hussein, even before CNN, the FBI and the CIA. Turi also feels that bin Laden is currently hiding in Iraq under the protection of Hussein and that the search for the terrorist will continue to be extremely difficult.

TURI STARTS TO QUESTION ME

After going over many of the details of his complex astrological methods, much of which I admittedly had difficulty understanding, Turi casually posed a question.

"What month were you born, by the way?" he asked.

"February," I replied.

"Like me. What year?"

"1958," I said.

"February 1958," he noted. "Let me check you for the dragon. Do you want me to do that?"

"Sure," I said, rather gamely I thought.

"Aquarius rules the future," Turi said, "television, radio, UFOs. I'm an Aquarius, too, so I know. It rules the stars also. All right. In astrology, there is nothing religious or folkloric. You have the head of the dragon in Scorpio, and you have the tail in Taurus, in your fourth house. Taurus means money, so you may be forced, with the tail of the dragon on the financial aspect of your life, to lose everything you own in life two or three times. Then you have the head in Scorpio, which is the investigator, the metaphysician. Scorpio rules the police force, the FBI, the CIA, corporate endeavors, metaphysics . . . ."

I tried to argue by saying, "All I am is a journalist. How does that affect me as a journalist?"

"Well, you're an investigator," Turi stubbornly insisted. "You're not a journalist. You're covering yourself behind the word 'journalism,' but you're not. You're an Aquarius. You're a promoter of the New Age. You're a promoter of the truth. You're a promoter of the stars. That's your fate. That's why you're dealing with me. So am I. In my career, like you, I'm a Scorpio. So I'm also an investigator. I investigate the secrets of the universal mind and I rebuild people. I rebuild their awareness. I'm turning people into the eagles. I get rid of ignorance, because ignorance is evil and stupidity. I free their spirits so they can fly like the eagles.

"I just explained to you," he said, "and you can barely follow me because you're not educated. You don't have the basic understanding of the structure of the universe."

I don't have the basic understanding of the structure of the universe? I mulled it over a second or two, and then decided that I'd been accused of worse before and let the moment pass.

"Osama bin Laden has the tail of the dragon, like you, in Taurus," Turi began again, in his rapid-fire, thickly French accented speech. "He never worked a day in all his life, but he has squandered millions because he got it from his wealthy parents. But because he has the tail of the dragon in the sign of Taurus, it also means that he doesn't like money. He thinks money is evil, but he has no objections on using money for evil. He is a Pisces, so of course he swims downstream, as does religion in the Middle East, which is a Pisces area, too. It's impossible for him to swim upstream toward the stars and to recognize that the church, the religion, is not the synagogue or Allah or Buddha but the universe. He doesn't recognize that. He can't.

"He's got the head of the dragon in his ninth house," Turi went on, "which rules religion. But he has it in the sign of Scorpio, which is the sign of death. Do you understand what I'm saying?"

I said I understood and the interview continued.

WHAT THE STARS SAY ABOUT OUR WORLD

Turi offered more in the way of geopolitical astrology.

"The stars affect every country," he said. "Leo is love, romance, and the arts, and Leo rules France and Italy. This is why we say the French are romantic. It affects our language, and it affects our personalities. Germany is an Aries country, ruled and controlled by Mars, the sign of war. The best steel in the world is to be found in the mountains of Bavaria, in Germany, where they also make the best tanks, the best weaponry. And Hitler was an Aries. Aries is the body and the 'new start,' and he wanted to start the Aries race, or the Aryan race. It's the same words.

"Of course when he visited the seven miles of secret library under the Vatican," Turi continued, "this is why he never really invaded Italy. He was friends with the pope, and he realized with the knowledge of astrology under the Vatican that his country was an Aries country and that he was an Aries, so he came back home and manipulated the wise German people and turned them into a war machine, because the country is a war machine. Even their accent is army-like, is very rough. In this world, Aries or Mars rules the army, the navy, fire, machinery, anything that is engineering, including the ingenuity of the Germans, their ability to produce weaponry. This is why, after the first and second world wars, the Americans and Russians fought to grasp the German mind so that they could use it properly.

"So it's all common sense. England is controlled by Capricorn, which is manipulation and politics. There is politics in this world because of the genius of the English to structure government. That's why they ran your country for a while. Japan is under Uranus, which is the sign of the release of energy, uranium, and rules electronics and computers and UFOs. This is why they are masters in producing high tech. And they have experienced the worst of this planet. Japan is the only country to experience the worst of Uranus, which is the sudden release of uranium, or an atomic explosion, like Nagasaki and Hiroshima.

"And the Middle East is Pisces," Turi continued. "This is why you have Christians who would die for Bethlehem, and just a few miles away you have the Arabs who would die for the Rock of Allah, the Muslims. And then you have the Jews who would die for the Wall of Lamentations right in the same area. Now in that same arena, you have that poison, that religious poison, that comes from the Middle East. And Neptune rules the oil, and that's why these countries produce a lot of oil. Neptune also produces religion and destruction in the process.

"You don't poison only physically with oil burned in the atmosphere. You poison the mind also with religion. How are you going to change that? You cannot change these people because they do not speak your language. They're speaking through water. They think through water. They're fishes. They're Pisces. They don't see the reality of things, so the only way to get to the cleansing is extermination. That's why you cannot stop them exterminating themselves. They can't stop. You will never be able to stop war in the Middle East. They have to exterminate their ignorance, because the results of many, many centuries of religious poisoning have blurred the psyche of this people. They don't live for themselves. They're in a world of dreams. And Allah or Jesus is their essence of life. They're deceiving themselves."

THE DEATH OF THE AGE OF PISCES

According to Turi, the Age of Pisces that spawned all the religious warfare in the Middle East is soon to pass from this world.

"The Age of Pisces is ultimately dying," Louis Turi states. "The age of ignorance and of religion being classified as going to a church or synagogue is dying, and it's being replaced by the new Age of Aquarius. Mankind has to wake up and free its spirit and realize again that the true church is the universe and that the true twelve apostles are a reflection of the twelve signs of the zodiac. And that is the ultimate religion that will bless the world and will bring the option for peace and harmony."

Unlike the selectivity of man's organized religions, Turi said, astrology includes everyone.

"You could be born anywhere in the world," he said, "with any damn religion and you will still have a set of stars. So you have your identity as a child of the universe. That's what mankind will need to realize.

"The fight is also taking place in the universe," he continued. "The true evil is actually ignorance. And if you bring knowledge to somebody, you raise that person's consciousness and his personal vibration. Then he understands. He's educated."

Turi also foresees a day when the entire world will speak one language.

"There's too many different languages," he said. "This is why Aquarius is forcing everybody to communicate with the Internet. There's an option to communicate now all over the world, and to grow and expand and educate on so many different levels.

"So the Age of Aquarius," Turi concluded, "is bringing that universal awareness, that universal understanding, that universal language down to earth. We all have to speak a very specific language and a real true language. That's Aquarius. That's us."

Chapter Twelve
Does Whitley Strieber Have The Key?

"In the end of this, the body of man is going to be transformed–not just the mind of man and the spirit of man. There's no spirit/body bifurcation. This looks upon the body and mind and spirit as all one thing. So that instead of an out-of-body experience, you might be able to just plain fly, as far as I can tell."

Whitley Strieber is a renowned abductee and the author of the groundbreaking bestseller ***Communion*** (1987) and its sequels, ***Transformation*** (1988), ***Breakthrough*** (1995), ***The Secret School*** (1996), ***The Communion Letters*** (1997, which Strieber edited along with his wife Anne) and ***Confirmation*** (1998). In the long and continuing story of his ongoing experiences with aliens he calls "The Visitors," what is perhaps one of the strangest visitations took place when Strieber was far from home.

Strieber had an experience on June 6, 1998, while he was on tour promoting ***Confirmation***, that he felt was extraordinary enough to build an entire book around. ***The Key***, the story of a conversation with a small nocturnal visitor in a Toronto hotel room and the revelations he delivered to Strieber in the early hours of the morning, was released in early 2001. Strieber decided to publish the book himself rather than make the editorial changes demanded by the major publishers he had shopped the manuscript around to.

The Key begins with a visit by a mysterious figure that Strieber still cannot define as either alien or human but who nevertheless gave Strieber the blueprint for mankind's future.

THE STAGE IS SET

In the Personal Journal section of his "Communion Foundation" web site, Strieber wrote a brief prelude to the hotel room visitation in which he talked about how encounters with the Visitors had slowed down to nothing for a long period of time.

"It had been twenty months since my last encounter," he wrote. "When we lost our cabin in upstate New York, my thrilling life of weekly and even daily encounters ended. I grew angry. I became bereft.

"Then I pulled myself together," he continued. "I had completely given up the idea of ever having another encounter when I had the best, the most incredible, the most

Whitley Strieber

stupendous encounter of my life. It was truly a marvel, and it has left me in a kind of spiritual whirlwind. What an extraordinary event."

When a source like Strieber speaks in those kinds of superlatives, there surely must have been some kind of significant event that merits the use of words such as "incredible" and

"stupendous."

I spoke to Strieber about this visitation that so fills him with wonder and awe, and this most recent story he has to tell involves not only the future physical and mental evolution of mankind, but the salvation of our souls as well.

THE STORY BEGINS

I asked Streiber to run through his experience.

"It's a really simple story," he began, "just in terms of factual material. I was totally asleep. It was the last night of my author's tour. And in the middle of the night, it was about 3:00 AM, there was a knocking on my door. It woke me up. And for some reason, what popped into my head was the thought that I had fallen asleep leaving the room service man standing at the door for hours. Why I thought that, I just can't imagine.

"It's like the thought was just planted in my head by somebody else," he continued, "because it was such an exceptionally stupid thought. I mean, why would that ever cross my mind? I rushed to the door. I said, 'I'm terribly sorry. I fell asleep.' I threw the door open and this man walked into the room. He was smaller than I was by a significant amount, to where the first thought that might have even crossed my mind was that he was a child.

"He looked odd," Streiber said. "He was maybe four foot eight to five feet tall at most. I then had a remarkable conversation with this man. The time we were together, it was just incredible. I didn't have the impression at all that he was an alien, although I don't know what that means anymore. He certainly didn't look like anything except a human being.

"But the things he said were just extraordinary, and with such authority and knowledge. There were also words that he would use that now, looking back, I don't know those words. I just remember them as kind of gravelly sounds. I don't know what they were. But these words contained huge amounts of information.

"It was a really strange experience," Streiber went on. "And an extraordinary one. After he left, I still didn't know who he was. But I do know that he was a person in possession of the most incredible knowledge that I've ever encountered in my life about the meaning of mankind. Where we came from, where we're going, what's happening to us and why."

A DIFFERENT KIND OF LANGUAGE

I asked Strieber more about the kind of language his hotel room visitor had used.

"The thing is," Strieber told me, "that every word seemed to have attached to it thousands of ideas. And I have, in my head now, the contents. I mean, it's like having the contents of somebody else's mind in your own mind. Or at least part of it. It's amazing stuff. It's about a totally new way of being human. And how we can reach this, and how the conditions of the future are going to be such that we will be able to reach this.

"It won't be a pleasant experience," he explained, "because the conditions under which the changes are going to take place in us are very hard conditions. But I did have the impression, and this was very powerful, that the present time is as important in terms of evolution of consciousness and life on this planet as was the moment when living creatures first walked out of the sea. This is a moment of equal or greater importance in the history of the Earth."   I pressed to learn more about the language the mysterious little man had spoken.

"It was English, most of it," Strieber replied. "He could have been American or Canadian. He didn't sound English or have a foreign accent of any kind. It was like every word had ideas attached to it that are now in my head. I don't know how to express it. Like the words were words that somehow unlocked something in my mind. I'm not real sure what it all means. But there are just vast amounts of information."

At the time, Strieber said he was playing a waiting game with the information.

"I wrote notes that night," he said, "and I have the notes. I have some other notes I wrote and sent to my editor a few days later. And since then, I've been sort of waiting. Because I've found that waiting is important in dealing with this kind of experience properly. You can't jump on it, because if you do jump on it, then you get all mixed up. At least I do. And I get into the problem of having my imagination fill in the blanks, and I don't want that. So I've just been waiting."

WHAT STRIEBER WAS TOLD ABOUT THE FUTURE

Our conversation next turned to exactly what Strieber had been told by the hotel room visitor.

"So he was telling you," I asked, "that this is an unusually critical time in human evolution, human history?"

"Extremely critical," Strieber answered gravely.

"Does that accord with the apocalyptic view?"

"Yeah, it does," Strieber replied. "It's not exactly an apocalyptic view, but mankind is in a crucible and it's getting heated up. We're going to go through something quite fierce over the next fifty to one hundred years. The new millennium is going to begin hard. I didn't have any impression that we were going to go extinct or anything, but I think we're going to get bruised. We're going to get knocked about the head and shoulders by nature.

"I'm pretty confident in my ability to foretell things," he added. "My prognostications have been pretty on the money for a long time now. So I'm confident that when I do [make predictions], that it has a certain level of accuracy.

"I can say one thing," he continued. "My book is primarily about a new kind of human self and a new way of being human. And the context in which it begins is a retelling of the past that is true, that enables us to begin by knowing who we were and who we have been. And to therefore be able to make steps into the future with a clear understanding of where we have come from. An understanding we do not presently possess."

The changes will be unbelievably far-reaching, according to Strieber.

"It's a very physical thing," he said. "In the end of this, the body of man is going to be transformed—not just the mind of man and the spirit of man. There's no spirit/body bifurcation. This looks upon the body and mind and spirit as all one thing. So that instead of an out-of-body experience, you might be able to just plain fly, as far as I can tell."

I asked how the little man had been dressed.

"It was black, dark clothing," Strieber said. "A suit with a jacket that was buttoned up to the collar and a pair of dark pants. He was sort of normal. I can't remember too much detail about the style of his clothing because I was really riveted to what he was saying and by interacting with him. And the fun of it. It was terribly fun. It wasn't a pleasant conversation, but it was exhilarating to have this happening.

"I was very well aware at the time of how extremely unusual the whole experience was. And he kept sort of giggling almost because he was, too. He was almost laughing at the idea that I was obviously so excited. And yet at the same time, the things he was talking about were pretty intense.

"There was one thing that was fairly extraordinary. He told me the date of my death. And he said, 'But you must keep this a secret, because if you tell anyone, then it is possible that it will change.' And that is very true. Because if I told that and it became public knowledge, maybe someone would decide to change it just to prove me wrong, you know, and blow my brains out. So it was a very interesting thing.

"But I've had that happen before," he continued. "I was told the day of my death by the Visitors sometime ago and the day came and passed and I didn't die. So whether that is something to be believed or not, I don't know. In other words, when he told me the day of my death, he really told me nothing, because I've been told that, and it turned out not to be true. I lived for years expecting to die on that day, and it came and went and was a perfectly ordinary day. I didn't even skip a beat."

Strieber is not convinced that the little man was just another alien, however.

"The appearance of this man in my life was something of a surprise," he said. "He was not an alien. He was a human being. I mean he was just as human as you and me. I don't relate this much to the UFO stuff because it doesn't seem to me to be related, though he talks about them a little bit in [the book]. Actually, he seems to say that they were rather dangerous. He wasn't particularly complimentary about them. He seemed to think they were catalytic, but that they were also exploitive.

"I've had the thought for years," he explained, "that the process of evolution would look very negative to a dinosaur, but to the creatures that survived the crash of the comet, it would have been in the long run a wonderful blessing. In fact, it was. So he seemed to kind of recognize what the negative side of that evolutionary potential, the appearance of something new in our world, suggests. He even uses the word 'exploitation' at one point. So it's a mixed bag."

Strieber even sounds strangely protective of his visitor.

"The man was awesome," he said. "He was this extraordinary man and I feel a little embarrassed at the idea of the stupid things that would be said about him, and already have been on the Internet in one or two cases. Somehow I don't want him to see that. I don't want him to feel that. If he's out there anywhere—and he probably is. He said he lived in Toronto. I just can't find him. That doesn't mean he doesn't exist, though, believe me.

"But you know, I thought to myself later, could I have been talking to a member of some secret society who had a lot of knowledge, some sort of inner-world person or something? He could maybe be a human being who lived in other worlds, or higher realms or something. Or maybe he was an angel or something. I don't know. But I do know that he gave me the task of producing this document. And will it be my last book? I don't know. But it would certainly be a fitting book to end my career with, that's for sure."

THE NATURE OF THE CHANGES

Much of what the nocturnal visitor had to say dealt with coming changes in the both the physical and psychological makeup of mankind. One result of those changes, Strieber writes in **The Key**, will be in the way we relate to the world of the dead, which we will come to access as easily as walking across the street to greet an old friend.

And God, we are told, "wants companions, not supplicants."

The combination of the two ideas struck me as reminiscent of one of the final verses of the **Book of Revelation**, 21: 3-4, in which the prophet declares, " . . . and I heard a loud voice from the throne saying, 'Behold, the dwelling of God is with men. He will dwell with them, and they shall be his people, and God himself will be with them; he will wipe away every tear from their eyes, and death shall be no more, neither shall there be mourning nor crying nor pain any more, for the former things have passed away.'"

A world where God dwells with man, in a sense makes man his companion, and a world where there is no more death, are surely the ultimate fulfillment of mankind's longing through the ages. Is the mysterious guest that Strieber entertained speaking along those same lines? Do we dare hope that the prophecy will come to pass in our own lifetime?

"The veil between the worlds can fall," the visitor tells Strieber. "The undiscovered country can become your backyard. There is no supernatural. There is only the natural world, and you have access to all of it. Souls are part of nature."

The visitor also basically imparts a cautiously hopeful prediction of the coming New Age, coupled with ominous warnings about environmental disaster and the life-destroying effects of mankind's decadence and greed. The similarities to what Diane Tessman and Judith Bluestone Polich and others in this book have had to say are obvious, and therein may lie a testimony to the truthfulness of their message: even though they all draw their information from different sources, the consistency of their predictions is nothing short of remarkable.

STILL, STRIEBER CONTINUES TO WONDER

Strieber still hasn't managed to put aside all of his doubts about the events of that night. After first experiencing problems assimilating what he knew to be a real event into his normal, everyday memory, Strieber next had difficulty writing down what had happened.

"Immediately I ran into trouble," he confesses in *The Key*. "These huge ideas, and new ideas, were even more elusive than I'd thought they would be. Where was the soaring sense of newness and assurance that had been there when we were face to face? Where was the excitement? I struggled for days. But it all came out sounding like a mix of warmed-over Catholicism and New Age mysticism. Me, very definitely, and not even me at my best."

The writing process wasn't his only problem.

"I go through all kinds of different levels," Strieber told me in our interview, "of questions about whether or not he was even real. But the fact remains, because I know I do that when I have extraordinary and unusual experiences, that I called Anne [Strieber's wife] the next morning and said to her, 'Never let me forget this. Right now, I know damn well he was real and it was an incredible conversation. Do not let me drop this.' And I tried so hard to drop it so many times. I gave up on it.

"I had to learn the taste of a voice inside myself that was not my own in order to find his words in a lot of cases. It was really hard to do, but to me a fantastically valuable experience. The things that don't fit the paradigm quickly come to seem like dreams after they happen unless you are protective about preserving them.

"I know that now from long experience," Strieber said, "and that was why I called her. And it was the right thing to do. Because she knows it, too, and she has kept me on the straight and narrow with this ever since that day."

Chapter Thirteen
Dr. Joe Lewels: Mysteries From On High

It is Lewel's contention that, far from being an invasion by hostile, bug-eyed aliens from another planet, what we are seeing as the new millennium begins is the renewal of our relationship with the entities who both created us and have stood guard over the planet and humanity ever since, guiding our evolution and striving to lead us away from our own destruction.

Among the many paradigms and models of understanding used to interpret the UFO phenomenon is an often overlooked but still crucially important approach to the subject: that the appearances in the 20th century of what seem to many to be alien spacecraft actually had their beginnings at the dawn of creation. What we moderns call UFOs were called the Clouds of Heaven (among many other names) by the ancients, and, in spite of our different choice of terms, humanity both then and now has struggled to make sense out of essentially the same mysterious manifestations of something much higher than we can readily comprehend.

In a brave effort to stand outside the ranks of both mainstream science and organized religion, as well as the majority viewpoint of Ufology itself, writer and researcher Dr. Joe Lewels released a book called *The God Hypothesis* (1997, Wild Flower Press). It is Lewel's contention that, far from being an invasion by hostile, bug-eyed aliens from another planet, what we are seeing as the new millennium begins is the renewal of our relationship with the entities who both created us and have stood guard over the planet and humanity ever since, guiding our evolution and striving to lead us away from our own destruction.

I interviewed Lewels in 1997, around the time his book was published, for Timothy Green Beckley's wonderful but now sadly defunct magazine *UFO Universe*, and what Lewels had to tell me remains fresh and relevant today.

WHICH IS THE REAL GOD OF THE BIBLE?

In *The God Hypothesis*, Lewels puts forth the argument that there is a huge difference between the God of the Old Testament and the later God who brought Jesus Christ into the world.

"I think the Bible speaks for itself," Lewels said. "You read the Old Testament and

Dr. Joe Lewels

you read the New Testament, and what you see is diametrically opposed viewpoints. In the Old Testament, you see a God who is a wrathful, vengeful, jealous God who is a warrior and who leads the Israelites into battle against their enemies. And who helps them to conquer and massacre and slaughter their opponents. In the New Testament, you see Jesus Christ, who preaches the exact opposite of that. He preaches turn the other cheek. He teaches love thy neighbor. He teaches love the Gentiles and treats them just like anybody else. He treats women as equals. Everything that the status quo Jewish community who believed in Jehovah of the Old Testament—everything that they taught is basically disputed by Jesus Christ. To me, that speaks for itself."

Still, I asked, the appearances of UFOs in both the Old and New Testaments form a thread of continuity between both concepts of God, do they not? Lewels based his answer partially on Gnostic scriptures written shortly after the time of Christ, scriptures that say the material world was created by an evil Jehovah while a righteous Christ entered the world through a different and much more loving God.

"I would just say that both sides use the same method of transportation," he said. "As far as the entities inside of [the ships], my conclusion is that those would be different entities. But I don't think it's my place to judge them or anyone else. I would say the situation is maybe more like the Gnostics said, the forces of light versus the forces of darkness. But they both, it would seem to me, use the same mode of transportation."

WHAT NAME TO USE?

Does Lewels automatically equate some aliens with angels?

"The issue here," Lewels said, "is the use of terminology. If we use the term 'angels,' people immediately assume that we're coming from a traditional religious viewpoint. If we use the term 'aliens,' they think we're coming from a traditional Ufology viewpoint. I don't know what the correct term is. Are they angels? Are they gods? Are they aliens? Are they all three? I really have to keep an open mind here. All I'm saying is that the things we're describing today as alien UFOs and alien abduction are really no different than what has been described in the past by the ancients.

"Now, who was using the best term to describe these beings?" he asked. "I really don't know the answer to that. I simply hesitate to use religious terminology simply because it has a very strong connotative meaning. When you use the term 'angel,' you can't get away from a religious connotation. When you use the term 'alien,' that's pejorative. I'm not sure what the right term is, but I do think that if you examine the current UFO phenomenon carefully, and if you examine the ancient texts, including the Bible, that you will find extraordinary connections, extraordinary similarities. Enough to conclude that we're looking at the same thing. That's my main point."

And how does Lewels answer those people who throw out the word "angel" and call the UFO occupants "demons"?

"I think that a lot of people who say that," Lewels began, "are just simply looking at it from one side. And when you use the term 'demonic,' then you really get into some negative connotative meaning that comes from a religious perspective.

"I prefer not to deal with it in those terms," he continued. "It's too pejorative, it's too negative. It's too easy to assume that any being who does not look like a human is demonic. I think that's part of it. There's a prejudice against non-human entities. They look at the grays, they look at the reptilians, they look at the insectoids and say, 'Well, they're not humans. They must be demons.' And I don't think we can safely draw that conclusion, that they're necessarily bad or negative. It may turn out to be that way, but I'm not ready to draw that conclusion myself."

WARNINGS GIVEN TO ABDUCTEES

Whatever name you choose to give to the UFO occupants, one of the most consistently reported events in the standard abduction scenario is that of warnings of future apocalyptic doom being given to the abductees, often in the form of visions of the Earth exploding.

When I asked Lewels for his opinion on the prophecies given to abductees, he said, "In my research, I have found that the people we call abductees have uniformly been given some kind of message that the world is in trouble. They've been shown visions of what the Earth should look like and the things that we're doing wrong on Earth. They're ecologically aware. They're aware of the bad things that we do to animals and other species. They're very cognizant of all this, and it comes to them from their experiences."

Lewels cautioned, however, that when an abductee recounts a prophecy of a specific event, very often those predictions are not reliable.

"I've had a couple of people," Lewels said, "who've called and said, 'I had this tremendous vision of a great earthquake that is supposed to hit New York, and it's supposed to happen in three months.' And then, when the time comes, nothing happens. I think specific prophecies of specific future events are very, very iffy and should not be relied on at all. Because I don't think the future is cast in stone. I think that what we're looking at are maybe probabilities. And sometimes those probabilities don't work out."

But still Lewels defends the abductees' prophecies on the grounds that they are conceptually accurate.

"In general terms," he said, "the information the abductees are receiving regarding the problems with the Earth's environment are perfectly in accordance with what science is telling us. We can see that the icecaps are melting at a faster rate, that the oceans are rising, that the globe is warming, that there's likely to be more and greater storms, that there's likely to be more earthquakes and volcanic activity. And I think that the bottom line of the UFO phenomenon is to get the message out that the environment of our planet is in really great danger."

BRIDGING THE GAPS

Lewels told me that he wrote his book to bridge the gaps between mainstream religion, Ufology, and numerous other fields of study.

"I have found that some UFO researchers," he said, "have never read the Bible. They're ignorant about the Bible and they've never had any religious training. So they don't see how to relate what they're seeing and finding in the UFO field to religious doctrine. At the same time, most of the people who are theologians, people in the church, are totally ignorant of the UFO phenomenon. All they know is what they see on TV, or maybe they've read one book. But they're really ignorant.

"So somebody," he concluded, "has to have a perspective from both sides. If you don't have the perspective of knowing what the latest findings in quantum physics are, if you don't have a good handle on anthropology, psychology, comparative religions, and Ufology, then you're never going to have the perspective to understand this phenomenon or the true nature of reality or the true nature of God."

Chapter Fourteen
The Mid-East Crisis And The Future Of The Holy Land

Psalm 83: 1-8 (Revised Standard Version)
O God, do not keep silence; do not hold thy peace or be still, O God! For lo, thy enemies are in tumult; those who hate thee have raised their heads. They lay crafty plans against thy people; they consult together against thy protected ones. They say, "Come, let us wipe them out as a nation; let the name of Israel be remembered no more!" Yea, they conspire with one accord; against thee they make a covenant—the tents of Edom and the Ishmaelites, Moab and the Hagrites, Gebal and Ammon and Amalek, Philistia with the inhabitants of Tyre; Assyria also has joined them; they are the strong arm of the children of Lot.

As the final sections of this book were being written, the situation in the Middle East was quickly reaching a breaking point where the possibility of all out war seemed more immediate than ever before. Suicide bombings were epidemic and Yasser Arafat was a prisoner in his own headquarters in April of 2002, when I conducted a second interview with Biblical prophecy expert Gary Stearman. Stearman picked up where our first interview had concluded, moving directly to some key verses in Psalm 83, which are quoted above, and explaining his belief that Arafat is not really the primary enemy that Israel must deal with.

Stearman said that in 1982, an attempt was made to dissolve the Palestinian Liberation Organization and Arafat was exiled to Tunisia.

"But in 1983," Stearman began, "with the help of the Arab League, he reformed the PLO before it had a chance to die. Everyone had pronounced Arafat dead at that time, but in fact he came back to life. The thing that enabled him to come back to life was the Western powers, because the Americans and the Europeans came to regard him as the only man capable of speaking for the Palestinian Arabs. And he was only too happy to take on that mantle. And I think it's fascinating that in Psalm 83—there is not a clearer statement of the real enemies of Israel in all the Old Testament.

"Now people focus on Yasser Arafat as the enemy," he continued, "but I think of Arafat as a figurehead for the Arab League. The Arab League formed the Palestinian Covenant in 1968, when the PLO was born. And Article Nine of the Palestinian Covenant states, 'Armed struggle is the only way to liberate Palestine . . .' And then Article Fifteen says, 'The liberation of Palestine from the Arab viewpoint is a national duty, to repulse the Zionist, Imperialist invasion from the great Arab homeland, and to purge the Zionist presence from Palestine.'

"So essentially, from the foundational days of the PLO right on through Arafat's defeat and reformation in 1983, their central stated goal was the elimination of what they called the 'Zionist presence' in Palestine. Which of course means no more Israel—the final solution, as the Nazis put it.

"With that in mind," Stearman said, "Psalm 83, which is a signal year in the life of the PLO, has that verse, 'They have taken crafty counsel against thy people.' That's verse three. Verse four really states the Palestinian Covenant. 'They have said, "Come let us cut them off from being a nation, that the name of Israel may be no more in remembrance."' Then Psalm 83 goes into a list of the enemies of Israel. It is not simply the Palestinians.

"It starts out, in verse six," Stearman continued, "by saying, 'The tents of Edom.' That would be number one on the list. Well, Edom is the heritage of Esau, and the Edomites became the people known as Idumeans in the time of Christ. Literally, from the days of Jacob right down through the time of Christ, the Edomites were the archenemies of Israel. Then in the days of Jesus, the Idumeans, under the Herodian Dynasty, developed a very close relationship with Rome and became Rome's cooperative partner. To this day, the Jews have a saying which is three words long. They say, 'Edom is Rome.' Because right after the crucifixion of Christ and the defeat of the Jews, the Edomites or Idumeans all intermarried with the royal houses of Rome and went off to be the rulers of Europe.

"Second on the list," Stearman said, "is the Ishmaelites. The sons of Ishmael would be today Kuwait, the United Arab Emirates, Yemen and the Saudis. Third on the list is the Moabites, and that would include southern Jordan today. The Hagrites, Gebal and Ammon would be northern Jordan. And Amalek would be the northern tribes of the Arabs, who again were also the archenemies of Israel. During the days of the Persian Empire, the descendants of Amalek become the ruling classes of Persia, and that would include today's Iran.

"And then we have the word 'Philistines' used in verse seven. Philistia and the inhabitants of Tyre. The Philistines—of course that's what the Palestinian Liberation Organization calls itself. Then the inhabitants of Tyre would be today's Syria and Lebanon. The hezbollah, for example, operates out of Tyre with the help of Syria. Then verse eight says, 'Assur is also joined with them. They have helped the Children of Lot.' Assur is last on the list there. The descendants of Assur are from the old territory of Assyria, which would be northern Babylon and on up into the ancient territory of

Nineveh. Call it northern Iraq and eastern Iran.

"So literally, Psalm 83 lists the enemies of Israel, saying 'Come let us cut them off from being a nation.' And you'll notice that Palestine, or the Philistines, are fairly low on the list of enemies. The real enemy is the Arab League. Then the rest of that Psalm is an imprecation against those enemies and it's a prayer to God that He would destroy them supernaturally. Of course, that is Bible prophecy.

"The bottom line is that the world tends to regard Yasser Arafat and the PLO as Israel's chief problem. In fact, it's a much wider problem. The entire Arab League is the sponsor of the Palestinian Movement, and the Palestinian Movement is only a subterfuge designed, as it says in the 1968 Palestinian Covenant, Article Fifteen, 'to purge the Zionist presence from Palestine.'

"The chief arm of the PLO is called 'Hamas.' Hamas is the group with Arab League backing, and more particularly the backing of Saddam Hussein. Recent documentation has shown that the terror movement among the Palestinians is largely financed by Saddam Hussein, who launders the money through Greek banks and shipping interests, which is then transferred to the PLO and specifically to Hamas.

"And they have—you might almost call it a suicide mill, in which they take impressionable young men and women and, through a kind of cultic brainwashing, take them to the point of being completely dedicated to giving their lives for Allah. Then they send them out with bombs strapped upon themselves. So these kids are not doing it out of any frustration, but rather because they're being sponsored and schooled. And then when they die, their families receive a stipend from Saddam Hussein.

"But here's the interesting point," Stearman said. "Hamas, in the Hebrew, is the word that is translated 'violent' in the Bible. And in Psalm 86, which I think is a prophecy of latter day events, we read in verse 14, 'O God, the proud are risen against me, and the assemblies of violent men have sought after my soul, and have not set thee before them.' Now the word 'violent' in Psalm 86:14 is 'hamas'—the very name of the PLO's leading terror organization. I find that quite fascinating from a prophetic standpoint. What are the odds that a Palestinian terror organization would have this name that appears many times in the Old Testament to describe violent men who have risen against Israel?"

Stearman next made reference to Psalm 87.

"Its opening verses are, 'His [God's] foundation is in the holy mountain,' and 'The Lord loveth the Gates of Zion more than all the dwellings of Jacob.' Well, the Gates of

Zion refer to the Temple Mount. A brief history of that is as follows: Under the leadership of the IDF, the Israeli Defense Forces, the Temple Mount was captured on June 7, 1967. Twenty-four hours later, then Minister of Defense, Moshe Dayan, gave the Temple Mount back to the Jordanians as an appeasement, saying in effect, 'We now wish to live peacefully with you. Therefore we're now going to allow you to maintain your control of the Temple Mount.' Which they did.

"The Mosque of Omar and the surface of the Temple Mount was remanded to the Grand Mufti of Jerusalem. And so in what has been called one of the great historical mistakes of the 20th Century, the Israelis gave back the Temple Mount after winning it from the Arabs in a legitimate contest of war. And they gave it back.

"In the years since 1967, the Arabs have firmed up their presence on the Mount. They are even doing excavating and building there in order to build a pilgrimage center on the mountain. And they have now taken the position that the Israelis have no right to the Temple Mount and must never again be allowed to control it.

"Well, the heart and soul of Israel is the Temple Mount, which is called 'Zion' in the Bible. Therefore, the Zionist Movement centers around taking repossession of the Temple Mount. That is the core of the struggle. The core of the struggle is not a struggle against Israel [as a secular political state], rather it is a struggle against Zionism [a future theocratic state]. And Zionism by definition is possessing and rebuilding Mount Zion and specifically rebuilding the Third Temple. So Psalm 87, which is prophetic, proclaims God's love for Mount Zion. Now the contest, then, lies in that small piece of real estate in downtown Jerusalem—the Temple Mount."

I asked Stearman if he had any final comment before concluding the interview.

"The only thing that I would add at this point," he said, "is that Bible prophecy says, declares emphatically, that an international consortium of nations will, for a period of time in the latter days, take possession of the holy mountain. So far, that has not happened. The Arabs are dominant there, and yet prophecy says that an international consortium of Gentile nations must eventually take possession of that mountain.

"It's significant that the United Nations is now asserting itself in Jerusalem, and there are calls going out for an international police force to be brought into Jerusalem. This of course would be under the auspices of the United Nations. And if it happened that the United Nations began to patrol Jerusalem and develop a presence on Mount Zion, that would be a fulfillment of prophecy. And it looks as though that may happen."

Chapter Fifteen
A Cry To Prophesy

The Twenty-first chapter of Revelation begins with a beautiful promise: "Then I saw a new heaven and a new earth; for the first heaven and the first earth had passed away, and the sea was no more. And I saw the holy city, new Jerusalem, coming down out of heaven from God, prepared as a bride adorned for her husband."

It reminds you of the ending of Close Encounters of the Third Kind, the descent of the mothership, brightly lit and with a majesty unlike anything you've ever seen before.

You dream sometimes that maybe you were called to preach. Out in the distance, you hear a cry to prophesy, a voice calling from somewhere unknown. Verses from the Bible come quietly to mind, as though your memory was trying to build a sermon from them.

Some verses that particularly haunt you are from the Book of Amos, Chapter Five, Verses 18-20: "Woe to you who desire the day of the Lord! Why would you have the day of the Lord? It is darkness, not light; as if a man fled from a lion, and a bear met him; or went into the house and leaned with his hand against the wall, and a serpent bit him. Is not the day of the Lord darkness, and not light, and gloom with no brightness in it?"

It is an extreme irony that many of us who devote a part of our lives to studying the prophecies seem to always be in such a hurry to get there, to see the events happen in real time, as though it was just another church picnic awaiting us. When one considers all the terror that may lie ahead of us, we should be more than willing to wait patiently, to postpone for as long as possible what can only be the most frightening events ever witnessed in the long and troubled history of mankind.

You can see the Lord's point pretty easily really. Don't be in a rush to see the darkness he will surely judge the world with, no matter how stouthearted you may be feeling at the time.

HEALTHY PARANOIA

Another verse you can't quite seem to shake is from the Book of Micah, another prophet from the Old Testament.

"Put no trust in a neighbor," it reads in Micah 7: 5-6, "have no confidence in a friend; guard the doors of your mouth from her who lies in your bosom; for the son treats the father with contempt, the daughter rises up against her mother, the daughter-in-law against her mother-in-law, a man's enemies are the men of his own house."

It's a scary thought, scarier than most thoughts you have about what's going on in these post 9/11 times. There was a friend of yours who came over from Ireland to live in the paradise that is Southern California, a paradise at least to the world outside it. You asked her one time what it had been like to live with what the Irish still call "the Troubles."

"Well, for one thing," she said, "you never discuss politics with anybody, because you never know what side they may be on."

You even recall a bumper sticker you saw on one of your morning walks around the neighborhood that said, "We Must Stand Together. Report All Traitors!" You couldn't really know how seriously to take it. Report traitors to whom? The bumper sticker police?

A verse from Jeremiah has stayed with you more than twenty years.

"The heart is deceitful above all things," reads Chapter 17: 9, "and desperately corrupt; who can understand it?"

Great, you murmured dejectedly, now you can't even trust your heart to tell you what is right, like the movies and popular songs have told us for so long.

LET'S LOOK AT THE UPSIDE

Okay, you tell yourself. You've got the future apocalyptic doom. You've got the daily depression and paranoia. But let's look at the upside, eh?

The Bible also has its share of optimistic verses, verses that promise a better world to follow all the misery of the End of Time.

Some of the best are from the Book of Isaiah.

Isaiah 65: 17-19 reads, "For behold, I create new heavens and a new earth; and the former things shall not be remembered or come into mind. But be glad and rejoice forever in that which I create; for behold, I create Jerusalem a rejoicing, and her people a joy. I will rejoice in Jerusalem, and be glad in my people; no more shall be heard in it the sound of weeping and the cry of distress."

Considering how the daily bread of Jerusalem has been a bread of weeping and cries of distress and pain, the promise that God will eventually heal that pain is encouraging indeed.

136

There's another verse from the Book of Psalms that has always struck you as exceedingly realistic and believable. Psalm 126: 1-3 reads, "When the Lord restored the fortunes of Zion, we were like those who dream. Then our mouth was filled with laughter, and our tongue with shouts of joy; then they said among the nations, 'The Lord has done great things for them.' The Lord has done great things for us; we are glad."

You think that surely that is what the moment of our salvation will really be like. It will be so wonderful that we will think we are dreaming at first, that it simply can't be real. Then when the reality of it manages to penetrate our long-beleaguered minds, we will indeed laugh and shout for joy. You think of it often, the unreality of a dream giving way to true and genuine happiness.

A FRAGMENT OF NOSTRADAMUS

Of course it's all still a little bit complicated, you say. There are also some extra-Biblical alien factors to deal with before the whole picture starts to coalesce.

You have never forgotten a book you ordered by mail almost on a lark, not knowing the wisdom it would contain: The Untold Story: Nostradamus' Unpublished Prophecies by Arthur Crockett. The book's claim to present genuine prophecies by Nostradamus that were never part of his main body of work but which were nevertheless circulated among the European royal houses for centuries is a fascinating one, but admittedly impossible to totally authenticate.

But there is part of one of the unpublished quatrains that simply can't be a random hit on the dartboard of truth. "A new breed descends in gratitude," the quatrain reads, "Conflagration in the heavens. . ."

You think it is obvious that the reference to the "new breed" is intended to mean the hybrid children being bred by the UFO occupants. The alien genetics program is long established as being one of the primary reasons humans are being abducted. The familiar tale of the abductee lying on an examining table onboard an alien space craft while their sperm or ova are being harvested is one the most often repeated events in what researchers call the "standard abduction scenario."

Another frequently reported event is the "presentation" of an alien hybrid child to the human parent, who is often frightened and confused, but who also sometimes feels a bond of affection for the child, as though acknowledging that they recognize the ties of kinship even in so strange an environment.

You understand it all to mean that when the aliens are ready to present their hybrid creation to the entire world, the "new breed" will indeed descend from the ships in "gratitude," and we on the Earth awaiting them will also be thankful that a major threshold of our evolution has finally been crossed. You think that surely that is the solution to one of the foremost mysteries of the abduction phenomenon, one that a merciful God is patiently waiting to reveal to us.

THE HAPPY PARTS OF REVELATION

You start to cheer up a bit thinking of the hybrid children, and it leads to other happier thoughts. There are sections of the Book of Revelation that offer a great deal of consolation and contain wonderful predictions of a nearly perfect world.

The Twenty-first chapter of Revelation begins with a beautiful promise: "Then I saw a new heaven and a new earth; for the first heaven and the first earth had passed away, and the sea was no more. And I saw the holy city, new Jerusalem, coming down out of heaven from God, prepared as a bride adorned for her husband."

It reminds you of the ending of *Close Encounters of the Third Kind*, the descent of the mothership, brightly lit and with a majesty unlike anything you've ever seen before.

The idea that the holy city Jerusalem descends from heaven is repeated in verse 10, and the prophet goes on to describe it as being made of rare jewels and precious metals.

"And I saw no temple in the city," verse 22 reads, "for its temple is the Lord God the Almighty and the Lamb. And the city has no need of sun or moon to shine upon it, for the glory of God is its light, and its lamp is the Lamb. By its light shall the nations walk; and the kings of the earth shall bring their glory into it."

From our 21st Century perspective, it is perhaps easy enough to read all those details as being the ancient prophet's attempt to put into words an alien technology that even we at this end of history cannot begin to imagine.

The concluding chapter of Revelation, Chapter 22, begins with: "Then he showed me the river of the water of life, bright as crystal, flowing from the throne of God and of the Lamb through the middle of the street of the city." Again, the flowing crystal river could represent some kind of life-sustaining alien technology.

Verses three through five: "There shall no more be anything accursed, but the throne of God and of the Lamb shall be in it, and his servants shall worship him; they shall see his face, and his name shall be on their foreheads. And night shall be no more; they need no light of lamp or sun, for the Lord God shall be their light, and they shall reign for ever and ever."

There are repeated references to a supernatural source of light, which may in fact turn out to be simply another example of alien technology that the prophet could only express in the language and understanding of his time.

THE STRUGGLE MUST GO ON

You tell yourself that you should give yourself a little credit for having some faith in the future. Meanwhile, you struggle to get through the day with your soul intact, the same as everybody else.

There was an interview you did with Whitley Strieber a few years ago. He was talking about how his relationship with the aliens was a problematic and difficult one at best. He never quite let his guard down with them and he still felt he couldn't be sure about their ultimate intentions.

You tell him that reminds you of the true meaning of the name "Israel," as it was first given to Jacob in the Book of Genesis (32: 28) after he wrestled with the angel. "Israel" means "He who strives with his Maker."

"Right," Whitley said, "we are Israel."

You were always grateful to be understood at that moment.

You've spoken to prophets and students of prophets, and you don't know whether to flee from the crack of doom or start cheerfully preparing for paradise.

You again savor the thought that we're really all Israel after all, and you say a prayer for mercy because of it.

About the author

Sean Casteel received his BA in Journalism from the University of Oklahoma in 1985. He has written about UFOs, alien abduction and related phenomena since 1989. Currently, he is a Contributing Editor to the *American UFO Magazine*.

Acknowledgments

My heartfelt thanks to my parents, Raymond and Pat Casteel, my daughter Jennifer, and my brothers Chris and Tony, all of whose love and support have kept me going through many a difficult time. Thanks also to my good friends, Roy and Debra Buchanan and John Anthony Miller. And much gratitude to Timothy Green Beckley for coaxing me through the writing process with the patience of a saint, and to Tim Swartz for all his expertise in assembling the final book. And finally thanks to everyone who granted me interviews for the book and whose experiences and ideas may point to a better future than we can yet imagine.

--Sean Casteel

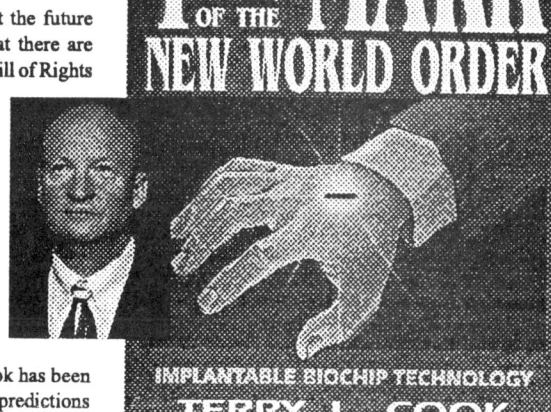
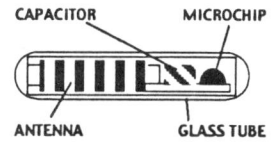